Mageborn

The Mageborn Saga, Volume 1

Dayne Edmondson

Published by Dark Star Publishing, 2018.

This is a work of fiction. Similarities to real people, places, or events are entirely coincidental.

MAGEBORN

First edition. March 13, 2018.

ISBN: 978-1386229810

Written by Dayne Edmondson.

Also by Dayne Edmondson

The Dark Tide Trilogy
Emergence
Eclipse
Ruin

The Mageborn Saga
Mageborn
The Cursed Tower
Halls of Light

The Seven Stars Universe
Ghost Ranger
Space Commando

The Shadow Trilogy
Blood and Shadows
Time of Shadows
Shadows Fall

Standalone
The Complete Dark Tide Trilogy
The Complete Shadow Trilogy

Watch for more at https://www.darkstarpublishing.com.

Table of Contents

Mageborn

The Mageborn Saga Book One
By: Dayne Edmondson

Published by Dark Star Publishing
Edited by Jennifer Ingman
Cover design by Rebekah Haskell

Typo Log

I want to extend a big thank you to the members of my ARC team who pointed out typos or other grammatical or spelling errors in this book:

- Edward Cooke
- Michelle Pan
- Cath McTernan
- Saundra Wright
- Richard

Prologue

Seventeen years ago

"Give up, you can't win," John shouted over the tempest swirling around him and his companions. The sun stood high above them. *I think it's high noon*, he thought. Too bad he didn't have a pistol to end this fight quick. Rather, too bad a pistol, even if he had one, couldn't end this. *Just a little longer*, he thought as his skin warmed.

Across the field, Valdorf stood, cape swirling behind him, clouds of shadow energy rising out of the ground and curling up his legs to envelop him. His eyes glowed red as he glared at John and the others. He pointed a gauntleted finger toward them. "You are more foolish than I thought." His voice boomed effortlessly across the battlefield. "Instead of fighting each other we could be ruling together. The mundanes of this world," he pointed upward, toward Tar Ebon and the Tower situated behind John, "are in need of firm guidance and strength. Who better to give them strength than mages?"

"This isn't the way to go about helping mankind, Valdorf. You risk destroying the world, not saving it!" *Have to buy more time, keep him talking.*

"Sometimes sacrifices must be made for the greater good. Like an infected arm being sliced off to prevent rot. What rises from the ashes will be stronger than what came before."

"Funny, I was just thinking the same thing about you. You're an infection, a plague on the Tower, a disgrace to the order."

"Enough talk," Ashley shouted from John's left.

John sighed. Hadn't she heard his thought where he said keep him talking?

Flames erupted around her in a whirlwind of red, orange, and yellow tinged with white. "Do you surrender, Valdorf?"

Valdorf threw back his head and bellowed a deep laugh. "Oh, such confidence. You think because you are chosen you can destroy what is beyond your comprehension. Let me show you true power!" He clenched the gauntleted hand into a fist and the seven gems fitted into it started to glow, like the colors of the rainbow. The ground began to shake, and a rupture split the earth in front of him. It spread in a jagged line toward the companions.

The wind rushed past John to swirl around and above Jason like a tornado. *Dude, I just combed my hair for this battle*, John thought.

Ashley nodded to her brother and slapped her wrists together while bending her hands in a cupping motion, as though she were catching a softball. The flames around her legs, body and arms channeled into the gap between her hands, forming a condensed ball of pure fire. She sent it rocketing toward the evil mage. The flames left her hands and she turned them downward and rocked back on one foot as a wave of pressure cascaded out in a cone toward the rupture in the earth. The ground rippled in front of her and met the crevasse formed by Valdorf's power, stopping its progress.

At the same time, Jason raised his hands high and focused the tornado into a thinner form. Ice formed in the walls of the tornado, increasing the lethality of the weapon and threatening to shred the target into pieces. He bent the cyclone and pointed it toward Valdorf like the maw of a dragon waiting to swallow its prey.

Thunder boomed overhead, and clouds materialized to the flanks of the sun. Lightning burst from the ground, surging through Alivia, and met every cloud. She raised a hand and directed a stream of lightning toward Jason's tornado, infusing it with electricity.

Here it goes, John thought as he watched the first strike. *Let this buy us some time.*

It might even work, Ashley said through their bond.

Oh, now you respond. You're not supposed to be the optimist.

Fire, wind, ice, and lightning surged toward their foe. First the flames, engulfing the man. No screams erupted from his lungs. Next the tempest came, obscuring John's view of the burning man as he imagined ice cutting him to ribbons, lightning frying his internal organs, and wind stripping the flesh from whatever was left and scattering the pieces to the wind. He closed his eyes, praying this worked.

It didn't.

An explosion of shadow energy erupted from where Valdorf stood. The fire, wind, ice and lighting hurled back like water in a puddle when a bridge drops into it. In the gap, their enemy stood, gauntlet still glowing, completely unscathed. Not even a hair out of place. He smirked. "Did you honestly think that would work? That basic elements could stop me?"

John shrugged. "It was worth a try. Tell her to get ready," he said softly in the calm following the literal storm, to Jason, who nodded. Almost...sunlight continued to stream into him and...there, he felt filled. "But now it's my turn." He smiled and focused all the sunlight in his body, and all around him, into a single point of light. It hovered above his outstretched hand. The sky and surrounding land went dark as midnight, as if a giant dome had covered everything but a small hole above John. Light streamed down like water through a funnel. The point of light grew. "Now!" he shouted toward Jason.

A cloud of shadow appeared a few meters in front of Valdorf. The cloud materialized into Bridgette, wearing her traditional black clothing, and Dawyn, wearing his now-traditional black armor. He held his dual blades, both as dark as the surrounding landscape, aloft to form an X. It was time.

John sent the light streaming toward the crossed blades, focusing it on the point where the two blades met. At first, nothing happened. John amped it up, sending *everything* he had toward the blades. Every ounce of light he could channel. He felt as if the sun itself would go cold with how much light he was drawing in. A chill ran up his back as even the light, and thus the heat imparted by it, within himself left to join the veritable army of light congregating in the dark blades. Finally, the blades glowed. First orange, then red, then finally white as they became the embodiment of his power.

The mage-forged blades retained their shape. As the stream of light winked out and the sun shone on the surrounding landscape, Dawyn separated the blades and held them to his side. What happened next, happened literally, in the blink of an eye. One moment, Dawyn was standing there, the next, he was in front of Valdorf, who had begun to lift his gauntlet to defend himself or strike Dawyn, with his blades hilt-deep in the man's chest.

Shadow energy streamed from their foe's mouth, which had opened in shock. "No," he croaked into the still air. "Im...possible."

Dawyn slid the blades out and Valdorf fell to his knees. Bridgette stepped forward and yanked the shadow gauntlet off his hand. She slipped her right hand into it and opened her hand wide. "Time to go," she said. Ribbons of shadow like that which possessed him earlier now lashed out like ropes to wrap around him. The shadow encompassed him and muffled his final words by slipping inside his mouth and down his throat. Then, when not a piece of flesh or clothing was visible, the shadow turned to mist and the mist evaporated in the sunlight.

John and Ashley let out a "whoop," Jason fell to his knees and Alivia stared blankly at the place Valdorf had been.

Dawyn sheathed his blades, now devoid of light and returned to their black form and walked toward the companions. "Good plan, John."

John held out a fist. "Fist bump."

Dawyn ignored the gesture and continued past John toward the city. "I will *not* fist bump you."

"One day you will, bro."

The knight just shook his head and continued walking.

Bridgette approached Jason, took his hands in hers, and brought him back to a standing position. She held his head in her hands and planted a long kiss on his lips. "I love you."

Jason smiled and looked down at his wife. "I love you too, honey."

John looked at Ashley and held his arms out wide. He raised an eyebrow.

Ashley just looked at him and shook her head. "Not when you're that smug."

"Oh come on." He threw up his hands. "I just, like, single-handedly saved the day."

"Good thing you're not wearing a hat. Your head might explode."

"Alivia will give me a hug. Won't you?"

The young mage blinked and shook her head to clear it, then focused on John. "What? A hug? Ummm...sure." She stood still as John approached and gave her a hug, but made no move to return the embrace.

Do you think she's okay? John asked through the bond mid-embrace. *I'll talk with her*, Ashley replied.

John met her gaze and nodded, then disengaged from the hug. *Yeah, some girl talk could do her good, I guess.* He offered a smile to Alivia, who had already turned her gaze down to study the dry ground, and turned his focus on Bridgette's hand. "What are we going to do about that?" he asked aloud, pointing at the shadow gauntlet.

"It's too powerful to leave laying around," Ashley said. "Can it be destroyed?"

"No," Jason and Alivia said in unison. Jason cleared his throat but deferred to Alivia. "The gauntlet cannot be destroyed by mortal methods. The records say it was forged in the heart of a void star."

"What the heck is a void star?" John asked. He hadn't exactly been paying attention much during their briefings about the coming battle. He'd been more interested in planning his heroic moves to get the job done. He thought at the time they could worry about super weapons later.

"It's the reflection of our sun in the shadow realm," Bridgette answered. "I can see it in the sky when I shift."

"But you can't reach it?"

"No. I haven't figured out how to leave the atmosphere or even leave the ground in that place."

"How do you know it's even possible?" Ashley asked.

"The legends the Founders left told of using shifting to bring the arc ships here," Jason chimed in. "It stands to reason shifting must work in space."

"Nice," John said. He snapped his fingers. "Oh, where did you send the V-mister anyway?"

"I imprisoned his body in the shadow realm."

"But I thought Dawyn's blades killed him."

"He wasn't human."

"We don't know what he was, exactly," Jason said. "We suspect he was part-human and part something else. He obviously had some control over the shadow realm for him to get the gauntlet from it."

"Was that info in the briefing?" John asked. He didn't think he'd missed *that* much.

"No. It wasn't mission-critical information," Bridgette explained.

"'This isn't spec-ops," Ashley snapped. "You should have told us what you were going to do. We thought Dawyn would just stab him, he would bleed out and die. Now you're saying you sent him someplace else?"

"It wouldn't have made any difference," Bridgette said stiffly. "I did what had to be done."

"You always do," Ashley muttered.

"What was that?" Bridgette asked, taking a step toward her.

"Whoa, whoa," John said. "Let's take it down a notch, ladies. You're sisters."

"In-law," the two said in unison.

John chuckled. "Jinx."

Nobody laughed before sobering. "Okay, okay, listen, big bad is in the shadow realm, it's done, it's over, he's dead." Bridgette did not contradict him, so he continued. "Let's talk about the gauntlet. What are you going to do with it?"

"I'm going to hide it somewhere no one will ever find it," Bridgette said cryptically. "It's safer if you don't know where."

John shrugged. "Fair enough. Take it away, Bridgette, and let's hope nobody ever finds it." He looked across the field to where Valdorf's followers were galloping away. "Should we chase after them?"

Bridgette didn't even spare them a glance. "They were worms thinking they would feast on the corpse of Tar Ebon, nothing more. Without this," she lifted her hand, "they're nothing."

"I hope you're right." *If you're not, humanity could be doomed.*

Chapter 1

"Ethan!" Emma shouted.

"What?" Ethan turned around, wooden practice sword in his hand. Sunlight reflected off his brown hair.

Emma idly wondered how her brother managed to keep his hair in good shape despite the north wind whipping down the narrow alley, heralding the coming of winter. Her own hair whipped behind her, probably making her head look like a tentacled monster. "Don't you remember what Dad said?"

"Oh come on! We're just having a little fun." As if conscious of her thoughts and her jealousy, he ran a hand through his hair. He then pointed his sword behind him. "Besides, Tam doesn't have a shot at actually beating me."

Emma rolled her eyes. Her brother tended to have an overinflated opinion of his combat prowess. A fact which had not escaped their father. "You're going to get hurt. Don't come crying to me, or Dad, when you do."

"Don't be such a worry-wart. You sound just like Mom." He turned to face his blond-haired opponent. "Where were we, Tam?"

"You were about to get beat, pretty boy, and your sister came to rescue you." He smirked, revealing crooked teeth. "I would listen to her. Run along back to mommy and daddy."

Ethan stood up straighter and his hand clenched his sword so hard the flesh turned white.

"Ethan..." she warned.

He ignored her, and instead added his second hand to the first and raising the blade high in the air.

Her idiot brother was going to get himself hurt. He'd be lucky if he only got a black eye, bloody nose, or some minor bruises. She clenched her own fists in frustration. Why did boys have to be so stubborn? Their mother always talked about "pride" and "honor", words usually accompanied by the rolling of her eyes.

Ethan swung his blade down with all his might. But instead of striking his opponent, the blade slashed through empty air and lodged in the ground as Tam side-stepped the strike and stepped on the blade.

"Too slow, mama's boy," Tam taunted. He swung his blade and hit Ethan's left hand, causing the latter to recoil and yelp in pain. "Or is it daddy's boy?"

"Shut up!" Ethan shouted, backing away and clutching his injured hand to his chest.

"Awe, did I hurt little Ethan's feelings?" Tam mocked, twirling his blade. "I thought you were almost a man. I guess you're just a scared little boy."

"Ethan," Emma shouted in warning. This was how he always got in trouble. There was a reason their father warned him specifically against fighting. He had a temper. And that was what bullies fed upon.

More boys and some girls had arrived, drawn by the shouting. They trickled down the sides of the alley and form two ragged columns flanking the boyhood battleground. Their presence had not gone unnoticed, either, for Ethan looked from side to side, his face growing redder. He straightened up, fists clenched at his side in wordless rage. So much rage for sixteen. Her father blamed it on something he called puberty, a time during which boys and girls, reached adulthood, while her mother said it was more specifically "hormones," or something in his blood which made him act irrationally sometimes.

"You don't even belong here," one of the onlookers, Zak, shouted. "Go back where you came from, southerner."

"I heard his mom was barred from entering the forges," one of the girls said loudly and purposely to her companions.

"His mom must be mental for even thinking she could work iron," another boy, coincidentally a forger's son, agreed.

Emma felt her own cheeks growing warm as she looked at the now hostile crowd. Like vultures come to feast, they had arrived to see their victim die, figuratively she hoped, and to devour what was left. But still, violence wasn't the answer. They had to...

With a roar, Ethan ducked his head and bull-rushed Tam. He was tall and lanky, while Tam was built like a bar of iron.

Tam braced himself and met Ethan head on, halting his charge with little effort. They grappled for a moment before Tam lifted Ethan up and whipped him over his shoulder.

Ethan landed on his back with a dull thud.

Emma resisted the urge to run to her twin, thinking of how *that* would look if his sister had to save him. He'd never live it down. But if she *didn't* intervene... She took a step forward.

Ethan sat up and started to rise, but slammed back as Tam kicked him in the face.

Emma winced. How could Tam kick a man when he was down?

Ethan didn't let the blow keep him down, however. He rose and stumbled back, clutching his nose, until his back hit the wall.

"Give it up, Ethan!" It had gone too far now. They needed to head home and cool down.

"No!" Ethan roared in a nasally tone, blood streaming down his nose as his arms went to the side. But this time, instead of charging, he closed his eyes. When he re-opened them they glowed white.

Emma stepped back in surprise. "What the..." she whispered, then shivered. Had the wind picked up? It felt as though the temperature had dropped several degrees in an instant.

Her brother's body glowed and streams of something like light, reddish-orange light, seemed to flow into him. She blinked and they disappeared.

For their part, the crowd nearest him backed away. Several of the girls hugged themselves for warmth. Tam turned to Emma. "What is your brother doing?"

"I don't know," Emma said absently as she watched the light show resume around him. The streams increased in number until she could barely see him. Idly, she noticed the light cast no shadow. Why had it disappeared for a moment?

The light sank into Ethan's skin and extended a hand, palm upward. A flame appeared, floating in midair, looking like a ball with a taper at the top. *This* light cast a shadow, and the shadows stretching behind Ethan darkened as the flame increased in size. He held out his other hand, where another ball appeared. An arch of flame connected the two balls a second later from both the top and bottom and her brother was wreathed in flame. It was like holding a candle before a mirror. He stretched his arms wide and the balls followed. The flaming circle stretched, arching higher above his head and scorching the ground before him. "Don't...talk...about...my...mother!" Ethan screamed. As if his breath had blown the ring of fire, it advanced toward Tam.

Tam, along with all the onlookers, turned and ran. Girls and boys alike screamed - all except Emma.

She felt a warmth originate in her stomach. It spread down her legs and arms and up into her head. The warmth evoked the feeling of the sun on a sweltering summer day. It felt *powerful*. The fire was mere feet away from her. She lifted her arms, hands splayed, as if by instinct, and braced herself for the attack. *I won't let you hurt anyone,* she thought. This wasn't him. This wasn't her brother. He didn't know what he was doing. A moment later the flame wall washed over her hands and continued up her arms and toward her body. She closed her eyes and imagined the flames disappearing. She had no idea how she, a nobody, could cause flames to extinguish without water. The warmth in her body increased, as if the summer sun were right above her. She opened her eyes. The flames were gone. She looked behind her, but only the crowd of onlookers, unharmed, greeted her gaze. Gasps came from several of them.

Emma looked down. Burns covered her hands, arms and chest. As if summoned by her gaze, the pain arrived, dropping her to her knees and forcing tears to her eyes. Her vision began to darken. Someone screamed. Then she realized it was *her* scream. A scream of agony. As she fell forward she distantly noticed Ethan, white as snow, toppling forward too.

Chapter 2

E mma opened her eyes and groaned as the pain hit her.

"Lie still, Emma," her father said, rising from a chair at her side and coming to stand in her view. "Don't turn your head or try to speak."

Despite the calm tone of her father's voice, Emma ignored the last command and tried to speak, but only a croak emerged.

"The flames seared your vocal chords. You have to let them heal." He glanced at her bandaged hands, which she was trying to lift. "Stubborn girl," he muttered. "I said lie still."

Her eyes widened. Panic set in as the memory of what happened crashed into her. Ring of fire, heat, intense heat, she...absorbed the heat. She locked eyes with her father and pleaded silently for help. Fortunately, her father seemed to guess her thoughts.

"Do you remember anything of what happened?" he asked.

Emma nodded and groaned as pain spiked from her neck.

Her father winced. "Sorry, that was stupid of me. Blink once for yes and twice for no. Okay?"

Emma blinked once.

"Do you remember how you got these burns?" he asked more specifically.

Blink. How could she forget? Her brother attacked her.

"Well, you're lucky to be alive," he replied. "Some neighbor boys ran up and said you'd been hurt." He averted his eyes and cleared his throat before looking back at her, eyes brimming with tears. "I feared you wouldn't make it." The calm in his tone was interrupted by waves of shakiness this time.

Emma looked down at her chest, which was covered by the same white bandages as her arms and neck, and back up at her father. How far had the burns spread?

Again he guessed her thoughts. "Most of the fire was isolated to your hands and arms, but some went up your arms into your shoulders, chest and neck. Your body just couldn't contain the heat effectively and you don't have the skill to diffuse it."

Diffuse? How was she to diffuse flames? What was he talking about?

"I carried you back here," he continued, "and applied salves to all your burns. I *hope* you'll heal back as good as new, but the burns were deep. You need rest and time to heal."

"Eth…" she croaked.

Her father closed his eyes for a moment before opening them and studying the floor. "Ethan is alive, but…he suffered severe hypothermia. He's in your mother's smithy being treated." He grabbed a pitcher of liquid and poured some into a cup.

Emma's eyes grew wider. Hypothermia, this early in fall? Yes, it was getting cooler, but it had been nowhere near that cold during the time of the fight. How could that have happened?

Her father opened his mouth, perhaps to answer her unspoken query, when a loud banging reverberated from downstairs. "Here, drink this," he insisted, putting the cup to her lips. After she took a sip of honey flavored water, he set it back on the nightstand. "You need to rest, honey. Let me deal with our…visitors…and then I'll come back up. Okay?"

Emma blinked. She *was* feeling tired.

Her father smiled, though it looked to be forced, before turning away, leaving Emma to rest in peace.

EMMA AWOKE AN INDETERMINATE amount of time later. It was dark in her room, with the only light coming from a lamp in the corner. It had been early morning last she remembered. Tenderly turning her head, she found no trace of her father. Panic struck her. Where was he? She croaked as she tried to speak. "Faa," she let out before her throat constricted. Distantly, she heard speaking from below her. Who was Father talking to? The voices cut off and she heard thumps as someone ascended the stairs. Seconds later the door creaked open and her father entered, also holding a lamp.

"Oh, you're awake," he said, noticing her head movement. "I'm so sorry, honey, I just went downstairs to speak with your mom really quick and to get you this." He gestured with his chin to a tray in his hands which held a bowl and cup. He stepped over and set the tray on the nightstand, then proceeded to lift the cup for her to drink from.

She sipped gratefully, feeling the cool water running down her throat and into her empty stomach, which took that moment to make itself heard. She swallowed and tried to speak. "How...," she stopped as coughs wracked her.

"How's Ethan?" her father asked for her.

She nodded and winced at the pain. She had forgotten to just blink.

"He's warming, and there doesn't appear to be any damage to his extremities. Your mother says he'll make a full recovery." He dipped a spoon into the bowl and offered broth to her. She sipped it and felt warmth spread down her throat this time, then opened her mouth further and he fed her another spoonful. He repeated this three more times and finished by offering the cup of water for her to sip from.

"What...happened?" Emma managed. Her voice still sounded hoarse, but the broth and water seemed to be helping with the tightness in her throat.

Her father pursed his lips and he looked worried. "With your brother?"

"Yes." Of course she meant her brother. What else could she mean?

"Well, I don't know all the details. But from what eyewitnesses told me your brother summoned and controlled fire."

"How?"

Her father cleared his throat and looked down toward her feet. "Well...darn it, I'm the parent here." He met her gaze. "Your brother manifested magic."

Emma was struck speechless, eyes going wide. Magic?

"He's the right age. According to the stories, anyway," her father added. "They say mages manifest their magic around the time they hit puberty. Sometimes the magic can lay dormant like...well like some mages...but other times it comes out right away."

"And me?" Her voice was still deeper than it usually was, but she could speak short sentences again. "How did I stop it?"

Her father sighed and shook his head. "That's the part you might not like. You, well, you drew the flames into your own body to extinguish the heat. You used your body as a heatsink and..." he stopped. "Sorry, I lost you there. Your body absorbed the heat but couldn't dissipate it into the air or another cooler source. So the heat manifested in burns on your skin."

Emma felt her head spinning, and not from whatever her father had given her to help her sleep earlier. "Do I have magic?" she asked, partially afraid to hear the answer.

Her father pulled at an earlobe. "It looks like it. The location of the burns and lack of burns on your clothing proves you weren't just a victim of the spell. You countered it...just the wrong way."

The wrong way? Was there a right way? How did her father know so much about magic? "How do you know this?" she asked.

"I knew a mage, years ago," he said, eyes focused on the far wall of the cramped room. "She told us about magic and stuff. I've sent word to her, actually, to help us."

"How can she help?"

Her father touched her shoulder gently. "We'll talk about that later. But trust me, she can help."

"Who was banging at the door?" she asked, changing the subject. It was clear she would get no more from him on that topic. Would the mage train them there at their home? Would they take her magic away? She had just learned she had magic, like the mages of the stories, and now they might take that magic away? That was a problem for another day.

Her father shrugged. "Just some angry townsfolk."

"Angry townsfolk?" Emma repeated, deadpan.

"Yeah." He waved a hand dismissively. "I sent them away. Though they might be back," he grumbled under his breath.

"What were they angry about?" she asked, fearing the answer.

Her father looked sheepish. "The people around here can be...superstitious. They don't understand magic and thus can become scared of it."

"Scared of me, you mean," Emma surmised. *And Ethan.*

"Yes," her father replied reluctantly. "Scared of your magic." He forced a smile. "But don't you worry. I won't let anything bad happen to you."

Emma felt her eyelids drooping and the pain in her arms returning. "I'm tired, Father. Please let me rest."

Her father smiled genuinely this time. "Of course, sweetheart." He kissed her on the forehead before exiting the room.

Chapter 3

E mma did not know how long she slept. Time lost meaning as she slept for prolonged periods of time, broken only by small fits of wakefulness during which her father, hearing her moans of pain, would rush up to give her foul-tasting medicine and a drink. He would then lay a hand on her shoulder and she could have sworn he would begin to glow before sleep took her again.

At last, after what could have been hours, days or weeks, Emma woke and did not feel pain from the location of the burns. It hurt to swallow her saliva, likely due to a dry mouth, but otherwise she felt better, much better. "Father," she croaked.

He didn't come.

She thought about moaning, as she remembered doing during her moments of wakefulness interspersing eternity, but didn't want to alarm him. Instead she pushed away the covers and swung her legs off the bed. She looked down and again saw the bandages like before, covering her chest, arms and shoulders. But they didn't hurt. She stood up and almost tumbled forward. But she caught her balance and took a step toward her door. She opened it and descended the stairs.

At the bottom Emma found her father behind the sales counter of their shop. He was dusting the counter and humming an unfamiliar tune. He froze when he saw his daughter. "Emma!" he shouted with glee. "You're awake! And moving!" He bustled around the counter, duster forgotten, and rushed to embrace her. Then he pushed her back and looked her up and down. "Let's get some clothes on you," he glanced toward the door, "before some customers come in."

"Water," Emma croaked.

Her father snapped his fingers. "Of course. Water, check." He rushed toward the stairs, then stopped and went toward the kitchen, then stopped again, looking conflicted. "Clothes or water first," he mumbled.

"I'll get the clothes," Emma said, her own voice grating on her. "You get the water."

Her father cracked a smile. "That's my girl, always thinking. I'm on it." He strode toward the kitchen, which lay beyond the sales counter.

Emma walked up the stairs, her legs threatening to cave beneath her. She donned a tunic and trousers, wincing at the tightness of her arms and chest as she stretched. She returned downstairs to find her father holding a steaming cup of tea. He proffered it to her and she took it gratefully, though she had been hoping for and expecting water. The first sip burned her mouth, so she took littler sips. Sometimes her father thought he knew what she wanted better than she did. She looked around after taking a third sip. The store hadn't changed. Weapons still hung on the walls of the large room, protected by thick panes of glass. Light armor, such as chain or leather, hung from racks filling the center of the room, while the heavy plate armor was displayed on manikins beneath the weapons. *At least the villagers didn't affect the store*, she thought.

"Where's Ethan?" Her father had said her brother was recovering well last they'd spoken of him.

"Still in the smithy, keeping warm."

"He's not recovering?"

"No, no, he is. Your mother is just cautious, that's all."

"Oh. Being a 'hypochondriac' again?" She smirked.

Her father put a finger to his lips melodramatically. "Shhh, don't let her hear you say that word." It was a word her father spoke under his breath sometimes, when their mother was going on about preventing this illness or that. She would glare daggers at him if she heard.

"My lips are sealed." She made a zipping motion across her lips. "But seriously Dad, did villagers really come to our door angry?"

Her father sighed and slumped, eyes drifting to the door. "Yeah, baby doll, they did. Not all of them, mind you, but a few of the more outspoken men in town."

"What did they want?" He hadn't told her before. "Did they..." she swallowed, "...want to kill us?"

Her father's eyes went wide, he straightened and he put his hands on her shoulders. "Nobody wanted to kill you. Trust me. If they had dared breathe a whisper of harming you I would have..." he stopped, "...well, I would have used one of my many weapons," he gestured to the weapons, from swords and daggers to maces, morning stars and axes, "to disabuse them of such a notion." He slapped a hand to his head. "Ugh, I sound like Jason, using big words."

"What did they want, then?" she asked, curious as to who Jason was but filing it away to ask another time.

"They wanted us to leave town."

"But this is our home."

"And that's why we're still here. I flat out told them no. Well, in more words than that...and meaner words...but you get the picture."

"They've always been jealous of Mom. That's what started the fight between Ethan and Tam."

Her father nodded gravely. "Yeah, the entire town is jealous of your mother. She's doing something nobody else in town could even dream about and that makes people nervous."

"Why *don't* we move? I mean, couldn't Mom be a blacksmith somewhere else?" *Somewhere warmer*, she thought. They had never traveled more than two days ride from Ironforge, but she'd heard of the southern lands being like summer all year long. She longed to live in such a place.

"She could," her father replied cautiously. "But she chose Ironforge for practical reasons."

"What practical reasons?"

At that moment the bell above the front door to their store dinged and a customer, a man with a long gray beard and blue livery, entered.

"I'll let you ask her yourself," her father said, smiling at the man. "I'll be right with you, sir." He turned Emma to face him and whispered, "There are two trays in the kitchen. Would you take them out to the barn for your mother and Ethan? Help yourself to some soup, too."

"Of course." She left her father to his customer and entered the kitchen. Two wooden trays sat atop the stone counter, a steaming bowl of soup and hunk of day-old bread atop each. She pulled out a tray and bowl of her own and glopped two spoonfuls from the iron cauldron hanging above the kitchen fire into the bowl. Then she pulled off her own hunk of bread and placed it on the tray. She picked up the first tray and left through the back of the house and crossed through the chill air to the smithy door. A table sat beside it and there she set down the first tray. Then she went back and grabbed the second, followed by the third.

At last, the trays staged in arms reach, she opened the door to the smithy. A wave of heat washed over her, causing her breath to catch in her throat for a moment. Panic threatened to descend upon her, like a thick wool blanket thrown over face, as she remembered the heat which had washed over her days earlier. She took an involuntary step back, trying to reign in her breathing. *Just stay calm*, she thought. *It's just Mom's smithy.* Taking a deep breath, she grabbed a tray and plunged into the furnace her mother practically lived in. An empty counter stood a few feet inside the door, and it soon became the resting place of all three trays after three trips inside and out. She kicked the door shut before looking around.

Her brother lay on a cot to her right, near the cooler side of the smithy. Only his head peeked out from beneath the thick blanket. To her left lay the entrance to the forges. The clang of metal on metal reverberated from the room. "Mom," Emma called. The clanging continued. "Mom!" Emma shouted.

At last, the clanging stopped. Seconds later, her mother appeared from the forges. Her red hair was tied back, soot covered her face, and the top of her head. She spotted Emma and smiled broadly, her straight, white teeth contrasting their surroundings. "Emma!" She stepped forward but stopped, looking down at her attire. Then her eyes fell on the food and she went to the wash basin and started washing her hands. "How are you feeling?" she asked as she scrubbed at her nails.

"Better. The burns don't hurt as much."

Her mother nodded. "Good. The salve worked."

"What was in the salve? Where did you get it?"

Her mother chuckled. "So many questions for someone who has been in bed for days. Aren't you hungry?"

Emma's stomach growled in agreement, as it had in her bedroom. Traitorous stomach, always interrupting important moments. "I suppose I am." She grabbed a stool and sat at the counter. Her mother came to sit next to her. She dipped her chunk of bread in the soup and gestured with her head toward Ethan. "What about him?"

Her mother took a sip of soup and made an appreciative face, her eyes scrunched close and lips pursed while she made an mmmm sound. Then she spoke, "He's still exhausted from his ordeal, but his body temperature seems to be normal now. We had to use blankets and the heat of the forge to warm him up."

"How did he become so cold?"

Her mother became somber and was silent in thought for a moment. "He drew heat from the wrong source to power his flame attack."

"The wrong source..." Emma started to ask. Then she snapped her fingers, dropping the piece of bread back to her tray. "Oh, from his body, right?"

"Did your father tell you that?"

"No, but he did tell me these," she gestured to her chest as a representative of all the burns, "were caused by absorbing heat improperly. So I just guessed the reverse could be true." A memory rose. "But I remember the air growing cold before he did it."

Her mother nodded, a far off look in her eyes. "Yes, he used magic to draw the heat from his body and surroundings and turn it into the wreath of flame every teenager who witnessed it spoke of. He could have killed himself. Normally the heat drawn from outside sources would be segregated to not affect body heat and..." she trailed off. "Well, I just know there is a proper way and he didn't follow it." She cleared her throat. "Did your father tell you we are asking for help from Tar Ebon?"

Emma nodded, unsure of what to say. Her father had said the woman was coming to help but hadn't said how. "He said a woman was coming to help us. Is she going to take our magic?"

"Oh, honey, of course not. She's going to train you."

"Here at home?"

Her mother averted her eyes. "Probably not. Mages are traditionally trained at the Tower."

"So we'll have to leave town?"

"Yes. It's for your own good."

Don't I get any choice in this? Emma thought. Sure, maybe they needed to be trained. But she didn't know if she was ready to leave home yet. But she held her tongue and just nodded.

They ate in silence, peppered with the sound of slurping and chewing for several minutes. Then her mother spoke, "Do you want to tell me what happened out there? Aside from the last bit about him using magic."

Emma swallowed and shrugged in what she hoped was a nonchalant manner. "Some boys were picking on Ethan. He got in a fight with one. They were making fun of..." she averted her eyes. "You."

"Oh, honey," her mother's voice exuded warmth and drew Emma's eyes to her. "You guys know you don't have to defend my 'honor' or such silly concepts."

You don't know what it's like, Emma thought. "Easier said than done."

"I understand."

Emma stifled a snort. "Were you picked on when you were a child?"

"No," she said, slowly, "but my brother was. He was...very smart...but also socially awkward. He didn't have many friends and so people tended to pick on him because he was different. But," she held up a finger, "I never got in a fight when people picked on him. There are other ways to resolve conflict than fighting. Most of the time." She said that last sentence under her breath.

"I didn't know you had a brother." This was the first time she'd ever heard of her mother having a relative. They'd never met their grandparents or any other relatives. "Is he still alive? Where is he?"

"He's alive, or was the last I knew. I don't know where he is, though. We chose different paths. He chose the sailor's life while I chose to stay on land."

"Are you angry with each other?"

"Oh no, sweetheart, I'm not angry with him."

"Oh."

At that moment, Ethan stirred. He groaned and opened his eyes. "Oh, hey," he grumbled, his eyes falling upon Emma.

Emma cracked a smile. "Hey. How are you feeling?"

"Warmer," he said, stretching and pushing off the blanket. "And starving." He put hand on his stomach.

"Well, get over here and eat."

Ethan rose to a sitting position and then stood, swaying. "Ugh, how long was I down for?"

"Three days," Emma and their mother replied in unison.

"What happened?" he asked, putting a hand to his forehead.

"Sit down, eat, and we'll tell you."

Ethan sat and wolfed down a bowl of soup. During the meal, his mother and sister filled in the gaps. Emma explained what happened immediately after he had summoned the flames and their mother explained what happened to his body.

"So," he began in summary, wiping soup from his mouth with the sleeve of his now several days old tunic. Emma wrinkled her nose at the scent wafting from it. "...I really messed up, didn't I?"

Their mother sighed and closed her eyes. "No," she said at last. "Well, yes, but no. You did mess up in that you let your anger, your emotions, get the best of you, but it wasn't your fault that your magic got out of control. It was mine. Mine and your father's."

"How is it your fault, Mom?" Emma asked. "You're not mages." Her parents may have been interesting, perhaps the most interesting in Ironforge, but they weren't mage-level interesting.

"No," she began hesitantly, a hesitation Emma found strange - her father had sounded similar, "but we could have looked for signs, had you tested, caught this before it manifested. Both of you could have *died*."

"Mom, this wasn't your fault." Emma placed her hand on her mother's arm.

Their mother withdrew a handkerchief from her trousers, wiped her nose quickly and rubbed at her eyes for a moment with the other hand before blinking and smiling. "You are both so caring. How lucky I am to have such caring children."

"What about the bullies?" Ethan asked. "Tam and the others. They called you horrible names. Mom, they made fun of you."

"I appreciate you defending my honor," she took Ethan's hand in hers. "But I am a big girl, Ethan, and I can take care of myself. Besides, I have your father for that."

"Why don't you work at the foundry?" Ethan asked, prompting Emma to make a shushing sound.

"Because I would prefer to work on my own. Away from the male chauvinist pigs in there."

"Then why did we come here?" Ethan pressed. "You said you knew people in Tar Ebon, some mage, right? Why couldn't you and Dad have lived in Tar Ebon or someplace?"

Her mother adopted an unfocused expression, indicating she was deep in thought. "Before we came here, I had dreams of this place. Not actual dreams, but daydreams. I imagined walking the halls of the foundry and working the great forges. I imagined creating masterpieces of iron and flame. But I was a fool."

"Mom!" Emma protested. Her mother was the least foolish person she knew.

"I was," she insisted. "Or at least I was naive. Naive enough to think my skill with forging steel could overcome the prejudices of the guild here. Could overcome the superstitions and traditions of old men afraid of what a woman could do. I tried. I marched into the forges and demanded they let me show them what I could do. I bullied them into allowing me when they refused. I showed them. I showed them one of my greatest works, or what I thought was, and still they rejected me. Dismissed me. Told me I would never be allowed to work the forges. So I left, but I didn't want to leave the town. No, I'm too stubborn for that."

Emma smiled at that. Her mother *was* stubborn, a fact her father lamented loudly at least twice a day.

She continued, "So we decided to set up a shop here. Your father volunteered to run the shop, I built a smithy in the backyard. People complained at first, about the noise or smell or whatnot, but I wasn't breaking any laws and and so they couldn't do anything to me. So here I've been, since before you were born, selling products to travelers from around the country while the foundry keeps its doors closed to me."

A sad tale, to be sure, Emma thought. It didn't surprise her - she saw how the sons of the foundry workers acted toward girls, but sad nonetheless. She felt the urge to hug her mother, to tell her it would be all right. But she had said she didn't need anyone to protect her honor. Giving her a hug wasn't protecting her though, was it? *Oh well*, she thought, rising and giving her mother a hug. Ethan joined in a moment later. "I love you, Mom," she said.

"I love both of you." She pulled back and looked them each in the eyes in turn. "And we *will* get through this, I promise."

Chapter 4

A knock came at the door.

"Emma, would you get that, please," her father called from the kitchen.

Emma, who sat behind the sales counter in her father's shop, hopped off the stool and went to the front door. If it was a customer, why hadn't they just walked in? She found out a moment later when she flung open the door.

A woman stood there, a burgundy coat covering her down to her ankles. Her hair was bright red and her eyes a light blue. Creases marked her face, stretching when she smiled. "Why hello, dear. You must be Emma."

Emma nodded, unable to speak. In the days since the "accident" she had remained inside, mostly, trying to avoid the other teens in town. She had failed a few times, running into "friends" who decided to mock her instead of showing her kindness. Others looked at her with fear out of the corner of their eyes as they almost sprinted by her in the street. Never had she felt so alone and helpless, but that all melted away upon seeing their visitor. "Please...please come in," she stuttered, stepping back and extending a hand. She had been expecting someone, but seeing a hero of the Federation on her doorstep was different. She hadn't known *this* woman was the one coming to see Ethan and her.

The woman, Alivia O'Leary, stepped inside and nodded to Emma, the smile never wavering. "Thank you, my dear."

"Who is it, Emma?" her father called from the kitchen.

"Ummm..." Emma began.

Her father poked his head out of the kitchen, perhaps worried at Emma's hesitation. His cautious expression morphed into a wide smile as his eyes fell on their guest. "Alivia!" he exclaimed. He came out of the kitchen, apron still around his neck protecting his chest, and rushed to embrace the red-headed woman.

Alivia returned the embrace and studied Emma's father's face. "Jo...Jeremy...it's so good to see you."

"You came sooner than we expected. If I'd known you were coming I would have prepared something more substantial." He gestured toward the back. "Well here, let me get Avery. How was your trip?" he asked over his shoulder as he made his way toward the kitchen.

"I figured it would take longer for the message to reach you than it would for me to just show up at your door," Alivia said. "The new steam wagons your...that Jason designed are quite amazing."

Emma's father stopped in his tracks. "There's a steam wagon that goes this far north?"

"Close. It stops in Galdreth. Then we took a carriage north from there."

"Hmmm, must be a newer thing. My clients didn't mention it."

"We were its first passengers on this route."

Her father nodded appreciatively. "I'm impressed." He pointed back over his shoulder. "I'll be right back."

As they waited, Emma looked over Alivia. She stood shorter than Emma by a couple inches, even wearing shoes with a few inches heel. Her blue eyes studied the walls, and the weapons upon them, the floor and the ceiling. At last her gaze came to rest on Emma. "How are you feeling?" she asked.

"Better," Emma replied, subconsciously raising a hand to her chest. The burns had continued healing and left minimal scarring. The bandages had just come off a few days earlier.

"Did your accident scare you?"

"Yes, it absolutely did" was what she wanted to say. She had been terrified more than any time in her sixteen years of life. But instead she shrugged. "Kind of."

Alivia smiled knowingly. "Well, I am glad you faced it with such bravery. We could use students like you at the Tower."

Emma swallowed hard. There it was, the mention of the Tower. Her parents had alluded to it but hadn't spoken of it much since the days immediately following the accident. When she had asked about the Tower and them going there they had told her to wait until their visitor arrived and all her questions would be answered. Well, the visitor was here, where were Emma's questions? "Yeah," she said in a non-committal tone.

"Is it always so cold here?" Alivia shivered. "I'm used to a slightly warmer climate in Tar Ebon, especially at this time of year."

Emma nodded. "Yes, it's cold often here. The wind whips down from the north and surges down from the mountains in the east. Luckily we stay warm."

"Yes, I am curious how that works. I feel warmth radiating from the floor. How are your homes heated?"

Had Alivia chosen this tangent because she sensed Emma's nervousness about any discussion regarding the Tower? Or was she genuinely curious? Either way, she welcomed it. "The foundry produces an immense amount of heat. There are pipes run through the ground that pass by the cellars of every home."

"Ah, hence the grid-like pattern of the homes. I wondered why they were built in such orderly rows and similar dimensions."

Emma nodded. "Yes, the builders of the city were smart." *If bigoted and chauvinistic*, she thought.

"So the heat travels through pipes and you have openings in your cellars?"

"Yes, every home has a grate which opens to a pipe that carries the heat. Some houses are on tributary lines, meaning they aren't along the primary path." Emma stretched out her hand, palm up, and made a circle motion. Then she made swiping motions to simulate lines coming out from the imaginary circle she had outlined. "Sort of like this."

Alivia nodded. "Ah, like roots of a tree, yes?"

"Yes." She hadn't thought of it like that before, but it was an apt description. "We are on a secondary line, meaning we're on a secondary pipe coming off one of the main pipes."

"So your house stays quite warm?"

"Oh yes. We have to close the grate in summer to keep from getting *too* warm."

"It does limit the expansion of the city, does it not?"

Emma put a finger on her chin. "I hadn't thought of that. I guess it would." Come to think of it, she hadn't seen any new homes built in her lifetime.

"A sign of limited forethought by the designers of this city. But then, they likely didn't expect the city to grow much at all. I find lack of forethought a common trait among humanity."

As opposed to what? Emma wondered. They were all human. Her musings were cut short by the sound of boots in the rear of the house. "Oh, they're back." She turned to see her father, mother and brother entering the main room.

Her mother smiled at seeing Alivia. "Alivia!" She moved perhaps even faster than her father had and hugged Alivia. "Oh it's good to see you."

"You too, *Avery*," Alivia said, smiling and winking. The way she had said her mother's name sounded odd. Like she had put emphasis on it when there shouldn't have been. Emma wondered at that. Could Alivia have forgotten her mother's name? Or maybe Emma was hearing things.

"Oh, I'm sorry, I got spots on your coat!" She exclaimed. Indeed, black splotches had transferred from her mother's blacksmith apron onto the red coat Alivia wore.

Alivia laughed. "Oh, don't worry about that." She wiped at the soot a couple times but otherwise didn't show concern.

"Well, don't just stand here in the doorway. Come in, come in," her mother chided Alivia as if she were a child. She led the way toward the parlor, which lay next to the kitchen and the storefront alike. There she pointed to a chair while she assumed a position on the large couch.

Alivia took a seat and focused on Ethan. "You must be Ethan."

Her brother nodded, too shy to say anything, Emma guessed.

"Forgive my appearance," their mother said. "Your arrival was a surprise."

"I already told her that, babe," their father cut in.

She gave him a look, the one with the raised eyebrow. "Well, more than one person can profess surprise, dearest."

He shrugged.

"So," Alivia said, suppressing a smile and looking to each of the four people gathered before her, "on to the reason I'm here." She took a deep breath and looked at Ethan and Emma. "Your parents sent me a letter. They told me about the incident, or accident as you called it, and what they *suspect* caused your injuries. I agree with their assessment based upon their descriptions. As such, I have a special offer for you." Again an emphasis on a word in a strange context. Of course they suspected. They weren't mages.

Emma's breath caught. *Here it comes.*

"I want the two of you to come to the Tower of the Seven Stars to train as mages." She kept her expression serious.

Emma exhaled. That hadn't been as hard as she thought.

Ethan, however, gasped. "The Tower? Really? Us?"

Alivia smiled outright, in what Emma saw as nervous, as if she had been as apprehensive as the teenager being asked the question. "You both have proved you have the potential, and while you're older than most students are when they start," her gaze drifted to their mother and father for a moment before coming back to settle on Emma, "...I believe you have the potential to become powerful mages. We can help you learn to not just control your power for safety reasons but *harness* your power to help society."

"Can't you teach us here?" Ethan asked.

"I could, but I have other duties at the Tower that take my attention."

"Like what?" Emma asked, curiosity warring with a desire to support her twin.

"Well," her gaze went to the floor for a moment before coming back up. "I am an arch mage of the Tower."

"So you're in charge?" Ethan asked uncertainly.

"Yes, I am one of the senior mages who oversee the administration of the Tower. One of my duties involves overseeing the curriculum at the Tower. That means," she said, obviously seeing the confusion in Emma's face, "I choose what classes are taught to the students and help develop them."

"Oh," Ethan said at the same time Emma blurted "interesting."

"So what do you say?" Alivia prompted. "Will you come?"

"How old are normal students?" Emma asked.

"Ordinary first year students are ten years old when they are recruited. We find that to be the age their powers manifest. But there are exceptions."

"We are sixteen," Emma pointed out. "Aren't we a little old to be trained?"

Alivia smiled. "You're never too old to be trained in magic." Again her eyes drifted to their parents. Was she trying to convince them? "I've trained much older students." Her expression brightened. "And I have two students with me now who are your age and starting their training also."

Hearing of other students her age perked Emma up.

"I think this is a lot to process," their mother said. "Can you give them an evening to think it over?"

Or a few days, Emma thought. This was a life-changing decision. "How long would we be at the Tower?" How long would they be away from their parents?

"Normal students spend seven years at the Tower. For you it will depend."

"On what?" Ethan asked.

"On how fast you learn."

Emma shared a look with her brother. They were quick learners, weren't they?

"Well, I will let the two of you think on this. I'm staying at the Cold Stone Inn if you need me. I shall return tomorrow evening."

"Oh, you don't have to run off," their mother protested. "Please, stay for dinner, I insist."

"I wish I could, but as I mentioned, I have students in my care. I left them with my assistant, so I should be getting back."

"Well, at least plan on it tomorrow, Alivia," their father said. "I insist. Bring the kids and your assistant - it'll be a party."

Alivia hesitated for only a moment before nodding. "Of course, I think that would be wonderful. It would give the children, I mean students, time to get to know one another also."

Their mother clapped her hands. "That settles it then. Good idea, Jeremy."

They exchanged farewells, including hugs, and Alivia departed.

Their mother studied Ethan and Emma, who stood still as statues in front of the sales counter, after the door clicked closed. "Well, what did you guys think?"

"She seems nice..." Emma began hesitantly.

"Do you really want us to leave?" Ethan blurted.

Their mother blinked. "Of course I don't want you to leave, Ethan. I'm your mother. It will break my heart when you go. But I know this is for the best. You need training or you could hurt yourself, or others, more seriously next time your magic gets out of control."

"Are you afraid of us?" he challenged.

"Ethan..." their father cautioned in a stern voice from where he leaned against the stair post.

Their mother looked aghast, mouth hanging open. "Honey, I could *never* be afraid of you. What makes you think that?"

Ethan averted his eyes. "You want to get rid of us so badly."

"We want you to go to the Tower not because we are afraid of you, kiddo. It's because we love you," their father said. "We want what is best for you."

"But we don't get a say in what's best for us?" Ethan asked. He looked at Emma. "What do you think?"

Emma took a deep breath. Now that he asked her. "Ethan...I don't want to leave Mom and Dad any more than you do. But," she pointed outside. Here it came. "...look outside. Our friends, or the people we thought were our friends, have turned their backs on us. We have no friends now. Or at least it feels that way to me."

"That's because they're afraid of us, Emma."

"That may be. But I don't want to live here being feared my entire life. Do you?"

"Well...well...we can change their minds," he protested.

Emma shook her head. "Do you honestly believe that?"

"So you think we should go?" he asked testily. "Just abandon our home and run off to Tar Ebon?"

"We aren't abandoning anything. We are *honoring* our family, Ethan. How many kids like us are there in the world, hmmm? How many with magic? I'm guessing not a whole lot. We are special, Ethan. I for one want to go someplace where I can feel special without feeling hatred from people around me or guilt for the gifts I have."

"Gift or curse," he muttered.

So that's what it came down to. Ethan didn't want magic, not really. Was he afraid of magic? Afraid of himself? Or was it something else? "How can you say magic is a curse?" She looked around to her mother and father, who remained where they were and wore somber expressions.

"Because of what it can do!" Ethan shouted. "Because of what I can do," he said quieter. "It can turn me into a monster."

"Oh, Ethan." Emma embraced her brother, eyes brimming with tears and a moment later felt arms around them as their parents joined in. They remained silent, allowing her brother's sobs to echo. "You are not a monster."

They maintained their mutual embrace for several seconds. At last Ethan broke away and wiped at his nose. He gave a shy smile. "Thanks, guys. That makes me feel better."

"Well, good," their father said. "But I'm sorry to interrupt this heartfelt moment with the announcement that I am *starving*. Who's with me?" He started toward the kitchen.

Their mother rolled her eyes. "Ignore him. He's a softy at heart." Truer words had never been spoken.

Chapter 5

The next morning Emma awoke and stretched, then washed her face and hands and made her way downstairs. The smell of eggs mingled with last evening's ham wafted from the kitchen. She entered and found her father facing off against smoke as he tried not to burn the eggs. "Ow, ow," he said, throwing the pan back onto the stove. Beneath, a fire roared. Emma shook her head. She expected her father would know how to cook by now. He'd been alive for what, a few decades?

"Did you get the fire too hot?" she asked with a smirk.

"Yes," he replied, distracted. He pointed at her a moment later though, a serious expression on his face. "But don't even think about absorbing some of the heat."

Emma's face fell. Would she ever live that down?

Her father, noticing the change in expression, smiled. "I'm just joking, princess."

"Oh." It hadn't felt like he was joking. "It's too early for jokes."

"Eh, I'm always so misunderstood."

"Where is Ethan?"

"Still sleeping. I haven't seen him come down yet." He pulled the pan off the stove again and used a metal spatula, of course it would be metal when his wife was a blacksmith, to scrape the eggs onto a plate. He proffered it to her. "So you get the honor of my first batch of eggs."

"Gee, thanks," she said sarcastically, taking the plate and sitting down only to stare at the dry eggs. "You make almost burning eggs an art form."

Her father shrugged and then bowed. "I do what I can."

"Mom at work already?" She knew the answer but wanted to make small talk anyway to avoid thinking about the decision she, along with her brother, would have to make later that day.

"You know it," her father gestured with a thumb over his shoulder in the general direction of the smithy. "That woman would work dawn till dusk if she could. Working on three suits of armor, no, four, and the associated weapons for some knights passing through."

Emma nodded. Not surprising. Their mother worked strange hours. Some days she would work, as her father said, from dawn until dusk, while other days she would not work at all. Her father explained it was because sometimes orders wouldn't come in. Her mother could only work if there were orders for things to be made. It made sense to Emma once explained. She imagined it must be stressful working a job like that where any long stretch of time without orders, and thus revenue, coming in could spell famine for their family. She staved off her own famine for the day by shoving bland eggs into her mouth and chewing. Better than nothing, right?

"Dad, do you ever regret coming here?"

"To Ironforge?"

Emma nodded.

He smiled as he remembered something. "Well, I remember I was against coming here, at first. You see, I wanted to travel the world, see the sights, have adventures. But your mom, well, she wanted to settle down and start a family. She argued we couldn't rightly raise a family and travel the world. Needless to say," he gestured around the kitchen, "I lost that argument.

"But that was actually a good thing. This place grew on me, fast. I kind of liked being an entrepreneur shopkeeper in a sleepy town like Ironforge. It was a pleasant change of pace from the hustle and bustle of Tar Ebon and reminded me of home."

"Where is home?" Emma asked. She had asked before while growing up. She expected the same answer.

He blew out a breath. "Wee, well," he scratched at his head, "home is very, very far away and well...it's gone now. Or at least I think it is."

"Gone? Like destroyed?"

"No, just...I can't get back there."

"You lost your way?" She hadn't asked that before.

"You could say that. I don't know the way back home, so yeah, I guess I'm lost. Sort of like a ship at sea trying to find an island in the middle of nowhere."

"Is that why you wanted to travel? To find your home?"

He smiled. "Part of the reason, yeah. Partly because I used to get bored sitting in one place for too long."

She decided to ask him another question while he was in such a talkative mood. Often he would wave off her questions about where he came from, so it was possible he would answer this next question. "What were your parents like?"

He opened his mouth and for a moment she feared he would shut down that line of questioning. That he would tell her to go do some chore or another and not answer her question. Instead he closed his eyes, as if conjuring memories. "My mother had long, curly hair and green eyes. She was much shorter than me as I got my height from my father. He was as tall as I am now and had night-black hair cropped short and brown eyes. My mother was kindly and selfless. She was always willing to lend a hand to anyone in need. My father was stern. I guess working long hours every day does that to a man. I think he cared, or I like to think he did, but he...well...he had an odd way of showing his affection. I wish..." he trailed off.

"What?" Emma pressed.

"I wish I could have said goodbye to them. They probably wondered where I ran off to."

"You left without saying goodbye?" She felt aghast at the thought.

"I didn't have any choice," he said after several moments of pained silence in which she swore a tear dripped down his cheek. He cleared his throat. "One moment we were home and it seemed like the next we were here in Tar Ebon."

Emma could relate. Time seemed to pass quickly at times. Why it seemed like only yesterday she had been ten. "I understand."

Her father smiled appreciatively. "Thanks, kid, I appreciate the support."

"Any time, Dad." "Any time" was a common phrase he said to them, and it felt right to use it now. "What about Mom's parents? Did you know them?"

He nodded. "I sure did. We grew up in the same town actually. Right down the road from one another. Went to the same school and everything."

A school? They lived somewhere large enough to have a school for students? "And what were they like?" she pressed.

"Almost the exact opposite of mine. Boy, your grandmother had a temper on her. It's where your mother gets her...personality...from. I could hear old Grandma Maureen shouting from a mile away at one of her kids or your grandfather. No sooner would the shouting begin than the front door of their farmhouse would slam open and out would pour the kids. Your grandpa would leave a few minutes later, perhaps trying to save face, and drive into town to grab something for the house."

"Drive? Drive what?"

Her father blinked. "Oh. Drive the wagon of course."

"Oh." That was a strange way of phrasing taking a wagon.

"So I have aunts or uncles. Because Mom had siblings?"

"Yeah, you do." He sighed. "But that's a tale for another day." He eyed her empty plate and then reached over, grabbed an empty water bucket and slid it across the counter to her. "Here, go fill this up."

Emma groaned. "Ugh, Dad! I wanted to hear the rest of the story."

"Go on, we need more water, kid. You mother's family is a tale for another time."

The mystery ate at her, but she did as commanded, stopping to don a coat before going out to fill the bucket. The sun was making its ascent while the north wind blew, heralding the coming of winter as it did so often these days. She expected they would see snow within a few weeks.

When she returned, her brother was sitting at the counter eating her father's second attempt at eggs. These looked far less rubbery than her batch. "The lazy bird gets the good worm," she said.

"What?" Ethan asked around a mouthful of eggs.

Emma shook her head, amused at herself but not wanting to explain the joke. Her father said if you had to explain a joke it wasn't funny enough. "Never mind."

"Did you both get your lessons done?" their father asked.

"Ugh, Dad, we have too much going on to think about math right now," Ethan protested.

"I'll take that as a no," he replied, pointing his spatula at Ethan. "It's due tomorrow."

"You're our teacher. You can make an exception."

"It's exactly because I am your teacher that I won't make an exception."

"Blah," he said, mimicking a phrase their father said often.

"What about you?" he asked, turning his eyes on Emma.

The lie swirled around in her head. "I...am mostly done with it." By mostly she meant perhaps a quarter of the way done. She would hurry through it that evening.

Her father smiled in what Emma felt was a knowing manner, but he praised her with a "good girl" rather than skepticism. Then he changed the subject. "Listen, I need some things from the market. You guys want to come with me?"

Emma shrugged. "Sure." It would be good to get out, even if it was getting cooler.

Ethan mumbled "sure" before slurping his water.

"Great. Then both of you go get proper clothes on and meet me down here in five."

Chapter 6

A short while later the three of them entered the market. Due to the higher elevation and cool weather prevalent in Ironforge for most of the year, the market was not an outdoor market. Rather it consisted of four buildings arranged in a square configuration. Four entrances, one in each corner, led into a central plaza ringed by the market buildings. They entered the grocery section, located in the northern building. Selections of fruits, vegetables and meat sat behind and to the side of a wide variety of vendor stalls.

Emma eyed the sword their father wore at his side. It was rare that he wore a sword. Was he expecting trouble? She was reluctant to ask, perhaps because she feared the answer.

Their father picked up an apple and inspected it. "Hmmm...it's mushy."

"It's almost winter," the haggard woman sitting behind the stall scolded. "You know this, shopkeeper."

"Maybe you could mash it up and make cider?"

"Do I look like an innkeeper to you?" she barked then cackled, causing Emma to shy away even though she knew this was only part of the banter between the two.

Her father ended up buying a small bushel of apples despite his observation. The woman was right - winter was coming and they couldn't be picky with any produce they purchased.

"Jeremy!" a man bellowed from behind them.

Emma spun to find a hulking, balding man with bulging muscles standing there, face red and glaring at their father.

The target of the man's fury turned calmly, leisurely, and surveyed the man. "Ah, Leeroy, isn't it? What can I do for you today?"

"Why did you bring your devil-spawned ilk with you?" he demanded loudly.

Emma felt her cheeks warm. Devil-spawned?

"Devil-spawned," her brother repeated, fists clenching.

Their father spread his arms wide, signifying encompassing the stalls in the market. "I wasn't aware it was illegal to bring my ilk, I mean, my *children*, with me to go shopping. Was anyone else?" he asked louder, looking around.

Most of the other vendors averted their eyes or tried their best to ignore the exchange. Conversations faded to whispers as vendors spoke to customers or fellow vendors. Perhaps their attempts at ignoring the exchange were really gossip-filled whispers.

"My boy Tam almost died 'cause of your kid," he shoved a beefy finger in the direction of Ethan. "We don't want their kind here."

"And who is 'we?'"

"You know who."

"No, really, I don't. If you have co-conspirators, let them come crawling out of the woodwork so I can face them too. Or are they cowards?"

"Ain't nobody 'round these parts a coward except your boy. Using magic to attack my son. Wasn't a fair fight."

"My recollection of the story is a bit different. You see, I heard that *your* boy and some of his, err, friends, decided to pick on my son. Bully him, if you will. He was protecting his mother's honor."

"Still don't change the facts," Leeroy said. "He fought dirty. It's not natural, I say, not natural at all."

"Would you care for a rematch?"

Ethan gasped. "Dad!"

What was their father thinking?

"Between the two of us," their father continued. "You and me, Leeroy, you and me. I win, you and *your* ilk leave my son alone. You win, my family and I leave town and never return."

Emma groaned. Mom would kill him if he lost this fight, then bury him and leave town. "Dad..." she began.

"I agree!" Leeroy bellowed. "Tomorrow at noon in the town square. You pick the weapon."

"Quarterstaff. I don't want anyone to die." Their father bowed. "Until tomorrow."

Leeroy stomped off and their father sighed. "I thought I left bullies behind in high school. I guess not."

"Why did you do that?" Emma asked. What was high school?

"Maybe I was tired of running," he said distantly. Then he blinked and focused on her. "Or maybe it's just time for someone to teach Leeroy a lesson."

"I don't need anyone to fight my battles for me, Dad," Ethan said.

"You won your battle, son. This battle is for the heart of the city." He must have seen the confusion in Emma's eyes mirrored in Ethan's because he went on. "Bullies like Leeroy think they own the town. They think they can insult people and get away with it without consequences. Everyone is afraid to stand up to them."

"What about turning the other cheek?" Emma asked. "Like in the Bible."

"Turning the other cheek doesn't mean standing by and doing nothing. No, there are times when good people, like you or me, must take action to prevent evil."

"You think he's evil? Leeroy?"

Their father laughed. "Maybe evil is too strong a word. But the point remains. Somebody needs to bring him down a peg."

If Mom doesn't bring you *down a peg first when she hears of this,* Emma thought.

Chapter 7

E mma's father ducked, and a flying pan flew over his head and smashed into the wall.

"You did *what*?" her mother asked, face red. Emma half-expected her to spew smoke from her nostrils. Or grab a hammer from the smithy.

Her father held up both hands and stood up straight. Brave man, as he was making himself an easy target for more kitchenware. "Well, I...honey, it's okay, I'm not going to lose."

"If you do," she said with a knife, a big knife, in her hand, "I will gut you, stitch you back together and gut you again."

He gulped.

"Mom," Emma found herself saying, then stopped mid-speech as her mother's glare turned on her. "Dad was doing the right thing." She forced herself to keep her gaze. It was like the time she had stolen bread from Old Man Hector's store, only ten times worse. "Leeroy..."

"That's Mr. Algier to you," her mother interrupted.

"Mr. Algier," Emma continued, determined to not abandon the embattled defense of her father, "is a bully. Someone needs to show him he can't get away with calling people names, insulting people and being a bully."

"And why does your father need to be the one to do it?"

"I...don't know." A truthful answer. She didn't know why she felt it had to be *her* father to face down the bully. "He's the only one who will, I guess."

"He's the only one trying to be a hero. Do you know what happens to heroes?"

"They get medals?" Ethan chimed in as he entered from the other room. Where had he been?

Their mother spared an exasperated glance for her son. "No, they get killed."

"He's just a street thug," their father said quietly. "No one is going to die tomorrow. Besides, we're fighting with quarterstaff, not swords. What could go wrong?"

"I've seen people use a quarterstaff to excellent effect," she replied. "Sometimes to lethal effect."

"Yes, but Leeroy is not one of those few people."

Their mother looked from her husband to Emma and finally to Ethan before sighing, setting the knife down on the counter and throwing up her hands. "Fine, I give up! You can go fight in a foolish duel, but don't come crying to me if you lose."

"And if I win?"

"Then I won't bring it up again."

He smiled. "Sounds fair to me." He extended a hand. "Shall we shake on it?"

She rolled her eyes and exited the house without complying.

THE SUN SHONE HIGH as noon came the next day. Emma's father approached the center square of town. He wore his ordinary green shirt and brown trousers and had decided against wearing a coat. Her mother and brother stood with Emma behind him while the onlookers stayed further back. A large crowd had gathered to watch the fight. It was likely the most exciting thing they'd seen in years.

Across the square, Leeroy approached. His son Tam, three other sons, and wife, who all the girls Emma's age agreed was ugly, stood behind him.

A nervous-looking twig of a man approached a point in-between the two men glaring at each other from a dozen paces apart. He carried a quarterstaff in each hand. He offered one to each of the men before clearing his throat and speaking so everyone nearby could hear. "We are here today to witness the duel between Jeremy Ellington and Leeroy Algier. Let any who object speak now or hold their peace." He looked around and, seeing no one raise their hand in objection, stepped back and raised his hands straight in the air. "Begin!"

Leeroy began, twirling the quarterstaff around and almost dropping it. Emma stifled a chuckle. Why had he agreed to a fight if he barely knew how to use the weapon of choice? Male pride, she supposed. The same reason her brother fought Tam instead of walking away.

Her father fared better. He didn't try to twirl his staff in any fancy patterns of designs. Instead he held it out to one side pointed toward the ground and waited. His stance suggested experience with the weapon.

Leeroy thrust his like a spear, stepping forward as if he were a soldier stabbing a foe on the battlefield.

Her father side-stepped the thrust and batted the staff to the side. His counter-strike sent Leeroy stumbling to the side and he took advantage of his foe's misfortune to slap him on the back with his staff. That turned Leeroy's tumble into a full-on fall. He landed face-first in the dirt, staff sliding several feet. Her father did not pursue and "end" the conflict, though. He simply stood watching Leeroy. "Do you give up?" he asked nonchalantly.

Leeroy struggled to his feet and spat, there was no blood there, then held the staff two handed like a Claymore her mother forged. "Never. You don't belong here." He charged, holding the staff he was pretending was a sword aloft.

Her father sighed loudly. "I did try to give you an out. Remember that." He charged toward Leeroy and at the last moment stepped to one side and swept out with his staff. It hit Leeroy's ankle and the man again stumbled face-first into the dirt. This time her father stepped up closer to his opponent and asked, "Do you surrender now?"

The man offered a muffled response and tried to rise. Her father didn't give him the chance. With a whack he brought his staff down hard on his opponent's back. Leeroy let out an oof and didn't rise.

Tam ran to his father's limp body. "You killed him!" he screamed.

Talk spread among the gathered onlookers. Was he dead? Did they have a murderer on their hands now? Technically it was a duel, but death had not been allowed in the rules.

"I did not," her father retorted, not turning around as he walked back to his family.

Indeed, a moan drifted from where Leeroy lay. Relief spread through the whispers of the villagers.

"The duel is done. Leeroy lost. Let this be a lesson for any other would-be bullies." He dropped his staff to the side and his eyes fell on Tam but then drifted to a group of tougher-looking men, well, tougher-looking most-often-drunk men as he spoke. Tam paid him no attention, but the men averted their eyes.

With that, they left for home.

Chapter 8

That evening a knock came at the door and Emma answered it. Alivia stood there, accompanied by a boy and a girl Emma's age and a tall dark-skinned man. "Good evening," Alivia said, inclining her head.

"Good evening," Emma replied. She studied the boy and girl. The boy wore his blond hair long, down to his shoulders and could've been mistaken for a girl if not for his broad chest beneath his gray tunic and strong-looking arm muscles. He looked her in the eyes and she was captivated by their blue color. He gave her a confident smirk. As for the girl, her auburn hair ran down to her waist and she wore strange-looking round pieces of glass held inside a frame of what looked like metal over her green eyes, eyes which exuded a warmth as she offered a shy smile before studying Emma's feet. Emma felt the urge to ask her what the strange invention was but then remembered her manners and stepped back. "Please, come in."

As the group passed through the doorway she got a better look at the fourth member of their group - a man with ebony skin and short gray hair atop his head. His weathered face looked from her to the sales counter and swept around the room, seeming to analyze everything he saw. He, unlike Alivia or the other two children, wore a purple robe with gold embroidery on the sleeves.

Her mother and father came out to meet their guests and ushered them into the dining room where steam rose from a delicious-looking ham waiting on the table. The rest of the side dishes quickly followed, ferried from the kitchen by Emma and her mother. They then all sat down to eat.

"Charles, it's been too long," their father said.

The dark-skinned man nodded his head toward their father. "Indeed it has, Jeremy. Too long."

"We haven't moved."

"No, it is I who is pre-occupied, I fear. The Tower is growing at a tremendous rate and it is rare that we venture so far north."

"In fact," Alivia said, "we haven't been this far north for over ten years."

"I guess Ironforge doesn't have many mages," her father conceded.

"Or they remain hidden," Alivia countered before taking a bite of green beans. "These are good."

"Thank you," their father said. "Family recipe."

Their mother shook her head. "No, the prejudice against mages is too strong here for there to be a secret order of mages."

The adults continued talking, but Emma tuned it out. Her thoughts drifted to what clothing she would pack and what she would need for the trip as she took a bite of the ham. Too salty for her tastes, but her dad enjoyed ham.

The boy, who had been introduced as Richard, leaned over and interrupted her thinking. "You as bored as I am?" he whispered. The gesture sent a chill down Emma's spine. He was cute.

Emma rolled her eyes. "Politics and gossip bores me," she said, doing her best to match his soft tone. Across the table, she saw Ethan laughing at something the girl, Jasmine, had said.

"What doesn't bore you?" he asked.

"Reading, drawing." *Daydreaming.* "You?"

"I grew up on a farm." As if that said it all.

"And? Surely you did things for fun?"

He chuckled. "I guess you could call wrangling pigs and riding horses fun." His face sobered. "I didn't have much free time otherwise. My da is not happy about me going away."

"He doesn't want you to become a mage?"

"No, he doesn't want to lose a farmhand. I'm the eldest and was going to be heir to his farm."

"Oh." Her gaze drifted to her mother. Had her mother wanted her or Ethan to take over the family business too? She shook her head. "Well, I'm glad he agreed to let you go."

"Arch mage O'Leary and Azek can be very convincing."

"I bet."

"Are you scared?"

"Of what?"

"Going to Tar Ebon. To be trained."

"No," she lied. "Are you?"

He smirked as if he had seen through her lie. "I think I would be a fool not to be at least a little afraid."

"Yeah," she agreed. "I guess I hadn't really thought about it." Truth time now. "I was more concerned with leaving my parents. I hadn't thought that far ahead yet."

"That's good you're close." He studied his cup. "My parents weren't, aren't, the caring kind."

Her mother did always tell her to count her blessings. She *was* lucky.

THAT EVENING, AFTER their guests had departed, Emma jested with Ethan before they entered their bedrooms. "Did you fall for Jasmine?" She made a kissing face. Ethan and Jasmine had laughed for much of dinner and gone off whispering in a corner afterward.

Ethan's face grew bright red. "I...shut up! You were making eyes at Richard too. I saw it."

Emma smirked. She enjoyed poking fun at her serious brother. "What did you two talk about?"

He looked even more embarrassed. "Frogs. We were talking about frogs."

Emma blinked. Someone else shared her brother's odd fascination with frogs? She voiced her disbelief.

"Yes, as a matter of fact. She grew up near the Highland Swamp, so she was surrounded by frogs."

Emma shrugged. "Whatever floats your boat." Another saying from her father, though no boats larger than rowboats sailed the river running down from the mountains. Ironforge was not known as a maritime city. Frogs always grossed her out. She remembered a time when her brother brought a frog home and threw it in her face. She hadn't slept through the night for a week as nightmares filled with giant frogs plagued her. "Are you ready for tomorrow?" she continued.

Ethan closed his eyes and looked toward the stairwell, toward where their parents still sat below, talking in hushed voices. "Yeah, I'm ready. Well, I have to pack some things, but..."

"I know what you mean." She took his hand, something she hadn't done since they were children crossing the street, and held his gaze. "Everything will turn out all right. I promise. As long as we're together we can do anything."

He smiled. "Thanks, sis."

Chapter 9

The next morning Ethan and Emma stood in the storefront, bags packed and travel boots which their mother had procured for them on their feet. She said the material would last a long, long time, though Emma was skeptical.

Alivia entered and looked them up and down before smiling. "Ready?"

Emma turned to their mother first.

A tear ran down one of her cheeks as she smiled broadly at her daughter. "I am so proud of you, Emma." She put a hand on each of Emma's shoulders and looked her in the eyes. "Listen. I know the journey will be rough at times and long, but I want you to know it will be worth it in the end. And your father and I will *always* be here for you. Understand?"

Emma nodded and hugged her mother for several moments before changing places with Ethan.

Her father wore his usual half-smile half-smirk as she came to stand in front of him. "Well, I guess this is goodbye, kid."

"No words of wisdom?" Emma asked in a serious tone.

He shrugged. "Make good choices."

"How do I know what the good choices are? And what if there aren't any good choices?"

"The thing I've learned is that there is always a good choice. It may not be the easy one, or the one you want to pick. Heck, most of the time the good choice *isn't* the easy one. If good choices were easy there wouldn't be so many people making bad choices. As to how to identify good choices, well, just ask what your old man would do."

Emma chuckled. "You don't always make good choices. Do I need to remind you about the duel?"

He waved a hand dismissively. "That wasn't a bad choice. That was a calculated decision."

"Is there a difference?"

"Yep. A calculated decision is a good choice that can go awry unintentionally."

"Don't let Mom hear you say that."

"Ha, you're probably right." His smile disappeared and he sobered. He raised his voice to be heard by Ethan too. "One thing I do want to mention." He looked to Alivia before returning his gaze to Emma. "There's a group, well, a cult really, that you want to be wary of. Sometimes they'll, well, try to poach young mages and turn them against their friends and family. Isn't that right, Alivia?"

"Yes. They're called the Cult of Rae," Alivia said. "They're a group of fanatics who hold many false beliefs, among them being that mages are somehow better than normal humans. Worth more."

"Alivia was telling us about them," their father explained. "Sounds like a bad group of guys and gals. So just keep an eye out, okay?"

"We will," Emma said, with Ethan mirroring her a moment later.

"Always protect one another," their mother added. "You are the best friends each other will ever have. Everything else could fall away but you'll always have each other. Never forget that, and don't let anything jeopardize what the two of you share."

"Wise words. Shall we go?" Alivia prompted.

Emma nodded and allowed the arch mage to lead her and Ethan out into the street where the two students and other mage stood waiting as a polite gesture.

"This way to the carriage." Alivia led them west toward the Iron Road. As they passed storefronts and villagers Emma tried to make a mental portrait of everything. She might not return here for many years, and a lot could change in that time. Some people stopped to stare at the strange procession, but most just carried on about their business, pushing through the biting cold of autumn.

A short while later they arrived at a carriage house near the Iron Road. Alivia gave a token to the man at the desk there who fetched the horses and hitched them to the carriage, then went upstairs and returned minutes later with a man in stained livery - their driver, Emma presumed.

"Oh, you're back," the driver said.

"Don't sound so excited, Declan."

"I'll have you know I was in the midst of a riveting nap."

"Well, your nap can wait. I trust you do not mind heading south to warmer weather."

"Bah, warmth is relative, you know," the man said as he mounted the carriage. "Spend six months at the Haguesfort and you'll know true cold."

"Have you been to Haguesfort?"

"Nay, but I've heard it's colder than a frost witch's tit up there."

"Watch your language," she scolded. "We have youngsters among us."

"Don't look like no youngsters to me. Look more like young adults."

"Are you two done bantering?" Charles asked.

Alivia blushed but nodded. Declan offered a bow, but Emma giggled like a child when he stuck out his tongue behind the man's back.

Alivia, the four students and Arch Mage Azek entered the carriage. It was a double compartment carriage, which allowed the students to sit in the rear compartment and Alivia and Charles to sit in the front compartment. Before they entered, Alivia explained it would take three days to reach Galdreth and the steam wagon that awaited them. As the carriage pulled away Emma kept her eyes glued through the rear window on the plume of smoke rising from the ever-burning flames of the foundry. *Goodbye*, she thought.

Chapter 10

The carriage rattled and bumped as it made its way down the Iron Road. Emma had half-expected it to be smoother, more like the name, but perhaps it was inspired by the roughness of raw unprocessed iron. She and her fellow students had spoken much over the past two days but now all three were asleep while Emma alone stared out at the fields they passed. Their father had never taken Ethan and her far beyond the bounds of Ironforge, so all of this was new.

They'd passed through two villages on their way south and stayed the night in each. Now they approached the third village Alivia said was named Farville. This village seemed larger than the previous two villages and more people were out on the streets though it neared dusk.

"Stop!" Alivia shouted angrily.

The wagon jerked to a halt as Declan responded to the angry arch mage's words. The door creaked open.

"Hey, wake up," she said in as loud of a whisper as she dared. She kicked Ethan in the shin.

"Ow," Ethan said, glaring at Emma. "What was that for?"

"We've stopped."

"And?"

Emma didn't answer. She opened the door and stepped out, searching for Alivia.

Charles was only just emerging from the carriage, wiping at his eyes. "What in the name of the Founding is going on?" he asked.

"I don't know, sir. Alivia ordered the carriage stopped and ran off."

"Maybe she had to use the bathroom," Ethan said from within.

Declan leaned his head over the side of the carriage. "She's up there." He sat straight and pointed in front of the carriage to the left, outside of their view.

Emma hurried to the front of the horses to get a clear view of where their new headmaster was and stopped. A crowd of people blocked her way. In the distance a round stake rose high above the crowd. A platform sat at the base of the stake and pieces of wood leaned against it. Were they planning a bonfire? She could not see Alivia. "Where is she?" she asked Declan.

"She's pushing her way through the crowd," he said. "I can see the top of her hood but that's all. Quite a gathering."

"Fool woman," Charles said. "What is she doing?" He rushed past Emma and was about to enter the crowd when movement on the stage caused him to stop.

A pair of burly men dragged a girl who couldn't have been any older than Emma toward the stake. The girl kicked and screamed, though the distance made the scream impossible to decipher. They threw her up against the stake and one pinned her there while the other tied her body to the wood with a rope.

Emma couldn't believe her eyes. She looked around for her companions and found her brother with the same wide-eyed look of disbelief she surely wore. Were they going to *burn* someone at the stake? A girl, no less? That was unheard of. Yes, criminals could be hung from the gallows or lose their hand or face other forms of punishment but never burning at the stake. And what did Alivia think she was going to do about it?

A third man went up on stage, this one holding a torch. The two men who had tied the screaming, and now crying, girl to the stake were using buckets to splatter something, oil perhaps, on the girl's dress and the wood surrounding her.

"Stop!" a voice boomed. Alivia's voice.

Emma looked around, for the voice seemed to come from all around her. Every member of the crowd looked around as well.

"Who said that?" came the much more distant voice of a plump man who ascended the steps and stood at the fore of the stage.

"I did." Alivia stormed up the steps. Two men tried to stop her but were sent flying backward to land on their butts. The action sent a murmur of "witch" through the crowd.

The man stared aghast at her. "And who are you to interrupt official proceedings of Farville?" he bellowed for the benefit of the crowd. In response, the crowed seemed to press closer.

"I am an arch mage of the Tower of the Seven Stars. I presume you are the mayor of this town. What crime has this young woman committed?" Her finger jabbed toward the distraught girl.

"She has been found guilty of witchcraft, and the punishment is death by burning."

"In what kingdom is that a punishment for anything? And what 'witchcraft' has she performed?"

"She poisoned my cows!" one man shouted.

"My crops withered when she walked through them!" another man shouted.

"She stole my husband away from me!" a woman shrieked.

On and on the voices drifted up accusing the young woman of evil deeds.

Alivia held up both hands to call for silence. "Enough!" she shouted when silence did not come soon enough. "Do you have proof of any of these allegations?" she asked the mayor pointedly.

"Well," he spluttered. "She obviously used magic to cover her tracks and remain hidden. That's the way magic works. All of these people," he gestured to encompass the crowd, "saw her doing these things."

Alivia pointed to the crowd. "You. The one with the cow. How exactly did she poison your cows?"

"She touched one of them, trying to milk it. A week after I ran her off my cows all fell ill and started dying."

"And was the cow she milked the first to die?"

"Well, no, but..."

"Then she obviously had nothing to do with it." She pointed to another person. "How long after she walked through your crops did they die?"

"A couple of days, ma'am. I caught her passing through my fields after she left them cows."

"No, ma'am, cows don't eat wheat."

"See!" the mayor bellowed. "Witchcraft."

Alivia shot the man a glare. "Your property is up against the cowherd's land, yes?"

"Yes."

"And did the grass near your wheat also die?"

The man didn't answer.

"Well, did it?"

"Yes," the man said in a much softer, far less confident, tone.

"Then could it not be that something *else* caused your wheat to sicken and die?"

"And what about my husband?" the same woman who spoke before screeched.

Alivia sighed. Emma suspected she knew she was running out of the time. For now the man with the torch had stopped in place but that wouldn't last long. A girl's life was on the line and Alivia was stuck playing detective. "What do you claim this young woman did to your husband?"

"She came to town and the next day I find my husband passed out at the bar rambling about a beautiful woman."

"Did he point to this young woman specifically? Was this the first time this happened?"

"Well, no, he didn't, but it had to have been a witch. He would never be unfaithful to me otherwise."

"Where is your husband now?"

"At the tavern."

"Then, my dear townswoman, perhaps the problem is your husband being a drunkard and not this young woman being a witch." She ignored the shouts of indignation from the woman and turned to the mayor. "I can stand here defending this young woman all day or you can let her go. Your choice."

Charles, who had been standing as still as a statue a few feet ahead of Emma suddenly spun around and yelled toward Emma, "Go back to the caravan where it's safe."

"But I can help," Emma protested.

"The charge stands," the mayor said. He nodded to the man holding the torch. "Proceed."

"Now!" Charles commanded before turning again to face the stage.

The man with the torch approached the wood and put the torch to it. The liquid coating the wood caught and spread in a circle around the mound of wood before encroaching inward. The young girl's tears turned to screams of pain and despair. Something silver around her neck reflected the light.

No sooner had the flames ignited than a ball of flame appeared above Alivia. Her arms stretched skyward as if holding the flame in an invisible cup. Streams of red and orange flowed from the wood toward the growing ball. Faster and faster the streams went until the wood turned to ash. Still the terrified girl did not burn.

She's redirecting the heat, Emma thought from the same position as before. Ethan and the others came up to stand beside her and watch the spectacle.

Moments later all the fire had transferred to the ball glowing above Alivia's head. A ring of ash now surrounded the prisoner. Alivia spread her arms wide and the ball of fire exploded in a wave of red and orange that spread across the sky in every direction for an instant before fading. Heat washed over Emma. The heat of the bonfire spread over the entire area, she guessed.

"Now," Alivia announced. "You will let this girl go."

The mayor stepped back, seemingly afraid. "She's a witch!" he shouted, pointing a shaking finger at Alivia.

Villagers in the crowd took up the cry of "witch."

"I am a mage," Alivia bellowed with the help of her magic. Her words cut through the din. "I did not deny that."

"Evil wench!" someone shouted. "Burn her!" another person shouted. "Her kind isn't welcome here!" came another voice. On the cries went.

"The girl can go, but you will take her place," the mayor said.

"Are you out of your mind?" Alivia asked. "I am a sanctioned mage of Tar Ebon and have done nothing wrong."

"You exist," a new voice broke out over the chatter. "That is crime enough." A tall man in a black cloak flanked by four guards in red ascended the stage and came to stand behind the mayor.

"Who are you?" Alivia asked.

"Rahman Aird, of the Shield of Man," he bowed not to her but to the crowd. "We defend mankind from dangerous magic-users like you, witch."

Alivia sneered. "Bloodcloaks. What are you doing so far north?"

"Evil exists everywhere," he answered. "It is fortunate for these kind villagers that we arrived when we did to put an end to the misfortunes that have befallen them. To shield them from the darkness."

"You probably orchestrated the misfortunes, you snake."

He smirked. "You see, dear people? The lies of a witch. What say you? Shall we do away with the witch?"

A roar from the crowd met his words. Charles cursed and pushed his way through the crowd. Emma considered running ahead too, or retreating to the carriage, but remained rooted where she was.

The red-cloaked guards accompanying Rahman spread out and drew their blades. Each of the men also wore a red veil which obscured his face. They moved forward.

Alivia backed up cautiously, angling toward the girl still tied to the stake but keeping her eyes locked on her assailants. The mayor ran off stage. Charles became lost in the crowd.

"What do we do?" Emma asked aloud.

"None of us know any magic," Ethan pointed out. Sure, Alivia had talked with them about meditation and the like the last two nights but none of the students had many any progress accessing their magic on command.

"And we don't have physical weapons," Emma agreed.

"We've got one weapon," Declan said from behind them. He rushed forward, and, in the fading daylight, Emma saw he held a crossbow. A short sword hung at his belt.

"You carry a crossbow?" Emma asked.

He spared her a glance. "Nothing deters brigands like a crossbow bolt through the chest of one of their number." He sighted the crossbow on one of the Bloodcloaks and released a quarrel. The bolt soared through the air and struck the main in the knee. His scream of pain was lost to the angry roar of the crowd and distance. Declan shrugged. "Or the knee."

Up on stage, Alivia summoned fire in her left hand, a small but growing ball. Emma thought she could see streams of something, like what one might see rising from paving stones in the middle of summer, forming strands and flowing toward her. Was she pulling heat from the air? Like what she'd done with the bonfire? Her suspicion was confirmed a moment later when a sharp chill replaced the warmth released by the earlier explosion.

The first enemy lunged toward Alivia and she threw a fireball toward his face. The man's head erupted into flame and his hands burned as they rose as if they could swat away or extinguish magic fire.

He stumbled to the side and fell off the stage. This caused a hesitation among the other two uninjured guards while the one with the bolt in his knee limped along behind.

Moments later people started to fly, only to knock into more people or hit the ground, away from one spot in the crowd. That spot repelling the crowd moved toward the stage. Emma assumed it had to be Charles. Her assumption was proved correct moments later when Charles bounded up the stairs to stand beside Alivia. He formed his right hand into a fist and held it up next to his face.

Declan reloaded his crossbow, but the crowd had begun to disperse, many streaming past their group, and his view of the stage was obscured. "Come on, kids," he said. "We have to get back to the carr... Get off my carriage!" he shouted. Indeed, several people had gotten inside and on top of the carriage. Someone whipped the reigns and the horses took off. "Shit!" Declan swore. "There goes our ride." He sighed. "Nothing for it then - toward the stage, but stay together!"

Toward the men with weapons who hate "witches?" Emma wondered. But Declan was right - they had no choice.

Alivia cut at the ropes binding the young woman to the stake with a knife while Charles maintained his previous pose. He bore no weapon, though, so what was he doing? He answered her unspoken question a moment later when he thrust his fist out and down in a punching motion toward one of the assailants. A second later that assailant shot backward as if hit by a battering ram. He slammed into the injured man and they tumbled across the stage. The last remaining enemy looked back at his fellows and then at Rahman, as if asking if his orders had changed given the unfortunate circumstances befalling the others.

"Don't just stand there," Rahman bellowed. "Get them!"

The guard charged toward Charles.

This time Charles swirled his finger toward the floor of the stage. A clump of leaves in that location rose into the air and swirled around like water around a whirlpool spinning down a drain. The swirling vortex made visible by the movement of the leaves collided with the guard and caught him in its grip. He spun around the vortex until the leaves fell and he flew off the stage.

By the time Emma and her companions reached the stage, Alivia had freed the young girl and helped her out of the ashes of the pyre. The girl met Emma's eyes with frightened gray eyes wide. Her soot-covered clothing matched the color of her eyes. She stood still as Alivia removed a silver collar from her neck and tossed it back into the pile of ash.

Alivia faced Rahman. "You lose, Bloodcloak."

Rahman smirked. "Ah, foolish witch, it's not that easy." He gestured to the direction Alivia had come from when approaching the stage. A dozen or more soldiers in red cloaks approached in the fading light. It had only been a few minutes since the fighting began, but already the sun was nearly gone from the sky. Rahman hopped down from the stage and strolled toward his soldiers.

"We can fight them," Charles said, huffing.

"I don't know if that is such a good idea," Declan put in. He held his crossbow with a bolt ready. "Some of them have crossbows."

"Which means if we run they'll shoot us in the back," Charles retorted. "I say we stand and...oof," his argument was cut short by a crossbow bolt from behind. He toppled forward.

Emma turned and saw more guards approaching from behind the group. At least a dozen. They were surrounded. Another guard lined up a shot. "Look out!" she shouted. The bolt streaked toward its intended target, Alivia, but Jasmine moved to intercept. It struck her in the chest. Her mouth opened in a wordless cry. Blood dripped down her chin, a red flower-like splotch blossomed on her tunic around the entry point. She crumbled to her knees and fell to the side. Emma guessed by the location of the bolt it had pierced her heart.

Declan fired a bolt in reply. It took one of the guards in the neck, though Emma couldn't tell whether it was a crossbow-armed guard or not.

Ethan and Richard went and relieved the two unconscious guards still on stage of their swords. She thought her brother looked silly holding a weapon in that moment, even though back home he used to practice in the backyard for fun when he thought no one was watching.

Alivia looked from the corpse of Jasmine, who had died protecting her, to Charles, who writhed in pain on the ground where he had rolled onto his side, to the soldiers both in front and behind them. It wouldn't be long before the next round of bolts came. "No," she whispered. "Not again."

"Alivia," Emma said. "Alivia, we have to run." Why hadn't the men on Rahman's side of the stage fired yet? She eyed them warily. Were they toying with them? Like shooting a cornered cat? She tugged Alivia's arm. She wouldn't budge.

"No." Emma thought she was repeating what she had whispered.

"But we have to get out of here." She tugged her arm again.

"No," Alivia said even louder. She shook off Emma's grip and took several steps away from her. "This ends. Now!" With that her eyes turned white and she thrust her hands skyward. Clouds drifted overhead, and Emma heard a strange crackling sound coming from them. Thunder? It didn't look like it was going to rain. Light flashed within the clouds as they darkened. Then, in an instant, the lightning connected with her fingers and Emma was temporarily blinded by a flash. She screamed. Had Alivia called lightning to herself? Surely she would be dead now.

She prepared to tell the others to run but stopped when she saw what happened next.

Lightning ran across Alivia's body. It flickered off her like sparks flying from a piece of hot metal when hit by a hammer. It curled up her arms like a snake and sparked off her fingertips.

Distantly, Emma saw Rahman pointing toward the stage and shouting something before running off into the gloom of evening. He at least suspected what was coming.

His prediction proved right as Alivia leveled her hands and lightning shot forth, spreading like tendrils toward the guards who had ambushed them from behind. It snaked around them and seemed to anchor them to the ground. Smoke rose around them. One of the men who tried to run was struck and jerked in mid-run before falling forward. The lightning strike continued until all the dozen or more men were dead. Unfortunately, the lightning had also started a fire. Houses near the site of the strike were ablaze. Villagers not already out on the street ran from the buildings shouting "fire."

Alivia continued her lightning strike, unconcerned by or unaware of the collateral damage left by her first strike, this time turning and directing her lightning to the group of soldiers where Rahman had been. This group, having seen what happened to their companions, had already split up and were trying to run. Alivia spread her arms wide and lightning crackled toward the outlying soldiers. She slowly brought her arms back together, catching any soldiers in her web of deadly light. A haze hung over the ground and Emma gagged on the faint smell of burning flesh. Her father had burned himself on a hot piece of iron in her mother's smithy once. He'd cursed for hours while her mother berated him for his carelessness.

The arch mage ceased her magic, her eyes returning to normal, and looked at Emma and the others. "It is done." Then she fainted.

"Declan, grab Charles," Emma commanded, taking charge of the situation. "Ethan, you get Jasmine," she ignored the pain in his eyes at the order to pick up the corpse of the girl he had a crush on. "Richard, grab Alivia. We need to flee." Even though most of the Bloodcloaks were dead, a fire raged through the village and the witch-hating villagers would doubtless want someone to blame. She looked to the girl Alivia had rescued. "What is your name?"

"Kylie Morrill," the red-haired girl replied.

"Lean on me, Kylie," Emma ordered.

"Which way are we going?" Declan asked in a labored voice as he hoisted Charles over his shoulder. She had asked him to take care of the heaviest of their group because she assumed a wagoner would be strong from lifting barrels. The fact he almost toppled backward on top of Charles made her reconsider that choice, though he stabilized a moment later. His crossbow hung on his back.

She summoned a map of the area in her mind, recalling the maps in her father's study. They might not have strayed from Ironforge, but it didn't mean Emma hadn't spent hours poring over the old maps. They had been traveling south, then gone east to where Kylie was being burned at the stake. Their attackers came from north and south. It was likely their path to both Ironforge and Galdreth was blocked or patrolled. Her gaze rose to the mountains towering in the descending darkness. "We go east." Perhaps they could lose their pursuers in the mountains.

Chapter 11

E mma and her companions moved as quickly as they could into the woods while the village in flames provided a distraction. She regretted feeling grateful for the destruction of the homes and livelihood of dozens or perhaps hundreds of people, depending on how fast the fire spread. After seeing how they treated Alivia and Kylie she squashed that feeling and focused on their destination. Which was...where? They could reach the mountains and follow it north to Ironforge or go south until they reached the King's Road. But she did not know how far the King's Road was and didn't want to endanger her parents in Ironforge, a town which didn't even have a wall to protect it.

The sun had faded from the sky and the bright full moon emerged before they reached the forest's edge. That slowed their pace more as they strove to avoid being tripped by roots or other hidden obstacles. Emma and Kylie took up the rear in case anyone fell behind. She kept looking back, squinting to see if anyone pursued them.

Some time later, when she could no longer see the glow of the fires or smell the smoke and as they were moving through a clearing, she called a halt. "We need to rest and bury Jasmine. And tend to Charles' wound." She knew enough from her father's stories to know an arrow remaining in a person for long was not good.

The three men set down their charges in the short grass of the clearing, Charles face-down with his head turned to the side. "I'll get a fire started," Declan said as he stretched and went to gather wood in the moonlight.

Charles groaned but did not stir, while Alivia remained comatose and Jasmine... Ethan bowed his head above Jasmine's stomach. Was he crying? Emma walked over to him. She squinted in the moonlight to see him. "Are you okay?" she asked.

Ethan said nothing for several moments, then lifted his head. "She died because of me."

"What? No, she didn't. You had nothing to do with it!"

"It should have been me who jumped in front of those bolts, not her. But I froze. I couldn't move. If I had moved faster, maybe..."

"Then *you* would be dead." Shame and anger warred inside her. She never wanted to see her brother die, so it angered her that he would suggest it would be better if he had died. But shame reared its head and she felt guilty for valuing her brother's life more than Jasmine's. She shoved both aside. "Look at me." She waited until he met her eyes, light reflecting off them. "The Bloodcloaks are the ones who killed her. They're the evil ones, not you."

He averted his gaze. "How are we going to bury her?"

She looked around but could find no tool to dig a hole with.

"I can help," Kylie said. She limped over and knelt, then placed her hand flat on the ground and closed her eyes. Nothing happened for several moments. Emma continued to stare at the space. She felt something like a shifting in the ground. Her head jerked back as the ground there shook, pebbles and dirt shaking.

The ground beneath Kylie's hand sank down, forming a hole, while her hand floated above. It grew wider, stopping at the tip of her shoes. She stepped back while keeping her hand aligned toward the hole. It expanded and then deepened, swallowing the light cast by the fresh flame created by Declan. She held her hand in that position for a few more moments before clenching it into a fist. The growth of the hole halted. "Go ahead," she said to Ethan.

Ethan stared at the hole before blinking and shaking his head. Had he been seeing the magic she used? Emma had felt something but couldn't see how she did it. "How did you...how did you do that?" he asked.

"You mean how did I learn magic?"

"Yes."

"I was trained from an early age."

"We have magic," Emma blurted.

"You do? I saw she did," she gestured toward where Alivia lay, having been dragged beside the fire.

"We are students," Emma explained.

"We've only used magic once," Ethan added.

Kylie cocked her head to one side. "You are a little old to just be discovering your powers. You never used magic when you were ten? That is when it usually manifests."

Emma shook her head. She couldn't remember any magical situations when she turned ten. Instead she remembered the doll her father made her, and the set of crotchet needles her mother made for her birthday. "We can talk about this later. Let me help you, Ethan." She went to the feet of Jasmine's body and lifted. Ethan followed suit and lifted her by the shoulders.

"Wait," Kylie said. She went up to her body and grabbed the pouch at her belt.

"What are you doing?" Ethan demanded, anger in his voice.

"Being pragmatic," Kylie replied coolly. "If she has money or supplies in this pouch we may need them. We lost our carriage, remember?"

"It's fine," Emma said, trying to cool her brother's temper. He was so much like their mother, letting emotion cloud his judgment. Once done, they shuffled to the side and gently placed Jasmine to rest in the magically-created hole. "Now how do we close it up?" she asked.

"Like this," Kylie said. "Pay close attention to see if you're able to sense what I'm doing." She thrust both hands out in front of her and spread them apart. Nothing happened. But Emma felt *something* in the center of the hole. Something she couldn't describe. Kylie brought her hands together slowly, as if they were pushing the dirt. The ground all around Jasmine's body stretched, filling in the hole. Emma searched for holes that opened elsewhere but found none. Somehow Kylie was creating more dirt. Or perhaps it was like taking dirt packed down by a boot and kicking it. Seconds later the gap containing the hole of their short-time friend was filled, replaced by a smooth patch of black dirt. "Well, did you feel anything?"

"I felt something," Emma admitted. "But then it faded."

"I saw," Ethan said. "You were manipulating the dirt to spread out. You compressed it earlier, didn't you? To create the hole."

Kylie inclined her head. "Yes. I reached out to the dirt. You will learn that in-between the elements making up all things there exists space. Tiny space, but even the most solid of objects contains space between its elements. A mage can eliminate the space to bring those elements closer together - to make something more solid. Or a mage can add space, or in this case, air, to expand something, like this dirt."

"So you didn't create dirt," Emma surmised.

"No. Dirt, or any element, cannot be created by mages. It can only change forms at our command."

The talk was making Emma's head spin as she tried to wrap her mind around dirt expanding and compressing at the whim of a mage. She looked toward the fire. "I should check on Charles and Alivia." She walked toward the fire where Alivia and now Charles lay. "Did you try removing the arrow from his back yet, Declan?" she asked.

Declan knelt beside Charles, studying the arrow in his back. He looked up and shook his head. "It's lodged deep in there. Without the proper medical implements I'm not sure he would survive me removing it."

Emma touched Charles' forehead. He was burning up and moaned. "Have you removed arrows from men before?"

"I'm not a soldier, I'm a wagoner, and sometimes a bard. He," he pointed to Richard, "would be more likely to be a soldier than I."

Emma swiveled her head toward where the farmhand sat looking sullen on the other side of the fire. "Do you know any field medicine?"

He shook his head but did not speak. Clearly the experience of the evening was taking its toll on him.

"Can magic heal him, Kylie?"

"It can," she began hesitantly. "But it is not my specialty. I could not stem the tide of blood long enough to begin the healing process. I was taught healing is one of the more difficult of the magics aside from control of light."

"So there's nothing to be done," Emma whispered. For the first time that evening she wished her father or mother were physically there. *I'm not strong enough for this.* "Can we give him some water at least?"

"We could if we *had* any water to give," Declan said. "Those hoodlums stole our carriage, remember? The carriage with our supplies."

Anger rose in Emma, but she took a deep breath to calm herself and measured her words before speaking. Everyone was just on edge due stress. "I remember, but I thought perhaps someone carried water on their person. Are there any streams near here?"

"Not near enough for us to be wandering in the dark looking for one, let alone trying to find our way back here," he retorted.

Emma swallowed a sarcastic reply but instead turned her attention to Alivia. Now was not the time for infighting. She placed a hand on Alivia's forehead. The arch mage was cold to the touch. "What is wrong with you?" she whispered, intending the words for Alivia. She understood physical injuries like what Charles had, but Alivia?

"She over-exerted herself," Kylie explained. "I've seen it at the coven sometimes. Usually a young student using too much magic at once."

"You're one to call someone young," Ethan chimed in. He had come to sit next to Richard and Declan on the other side of the fire. "You are what, sixteen like us?"

"Well, yeah," she replied, sounding embarrassed, "but I meant like twelve-year-olds."

"What's the cure? And what is a coven?" Emma asked.

Kylie frowned. "Rest and fluids was always the cure. And the coven...well...it's where I'm from. It's where witches like me are trained. I wasn't born there. I went there at ten."

Why do they call themselves witches and not mages? "We're out of water, Charles is dying, and we don't have time to rest." A thought came to her. Why had Kylie been in that village? "Where is this coven? Is it close?"

Kylie shuffled her feet and glanced away. "Sort of."

"Are we going in the right direction?" She grew frustrated at the sudden caginess of the girl.

"I..."

"You do not find the coven," a husky female voice spoke from behind Emma. "The coven finds you."

Emma stood and turned. A white-haired woman flanked by six other comparatively younger women emerged from the forest. Behind her, several men stood. "Do you know these women?" she asked Kylie.

"Yes. That is the grand matron, Seleste." Even as she spoke she performed a curtsy. "Grand Matron."

"Child. We heard your cries on the wind but feared we would be too late. How did you survive?" She stepped closer, revealing a wrinkled face housing kind eyes and a cane held in a gnarled hand.

"I was rescued by this woman," Kylie said, gesturing to Alivia. "And her companions." That gesture encompassed them all. "It was Bloodcloaks, Grand Matron. And they had the help of a dark mage."

The old woman pursed her lips. "A dark mage, you say. Were you bound?"

"Yes, they possessed Shara'han collars. She removed it."

"These are grave tidings you bring, child."

"Please," Emma interrupted. "The woman who saved Kylie, Alivia, she is a mage and she is unconscious. Can you help her?"

"A mage?" the grand matron asked sharply. "From Tar Ebon?" Her sharp eyes bored into Emma's head as if seeking the answers there.

Emma lifted her chin. "Yes. She is an arch mage of the Tower."

The woman's eyes narrowed. "And you?" Her eyes passed over the men and settled on Charles. "And these men? Are they mages also?"

Emma swallowed. "I am a mage in training, as is my brother and the other boy. That man there," she gestured to Charles, "was wounded in the fighting by a crossbow bolt..."

"Yes, I can see the bolt sticking out of his back," she interrupted.

"...and is an arch mage also."

"And him?" she pointed to Declan.

He held up his hands in an innocent gesture. "I'm just the wagoner. Sticking around until I get paid, and because I don't have much better to do, that's all."

The woman sniffed and returned her attention to Emma. "Where are you from, child?"

"Ironforge."

"You are old to be trained."

Why did everyone keep commenting on her age? They acted like she was sixty instead of sixteen. "We only recently manifested our powers."

"Ironforge you say..." she trailed off.

"Our mother is a blacksmith there."

One of the women behind the grand matron stepped forward and whispered in her ear. The grand matron listened, eyes never leaving Emma's face. She snapped something in reply and the other woman bowed deferentially. "You are in our woods now, girl. And you, and your companions," her face contorted into a slight sneer, "will come with us."

"Come with you where?" Fear struck in her heart. Why did the woman have such contempt for men?

"To the coven, of course."

"And the Bloodcloaks?"

"They shall not find us. As I said, the coven is not found - it finds you. Come." Without waiting for their acceptance she turned and strode into the woods. The other women followed.

Kylie made to follow but stopped when she noticed none of the others were walking. "Aren't you coming?" she asked.

"I've got a bad feeling about this," Ethan said. "Did you see the way she looked at us?"

"The coven," Kylie's face took on a pained expression, "has their reasons to distrust men, especially male mages."

"That doesn't make me feel any better," Richard said, arms crossed.

Horns blew to the west. "We don't have time to argue," Declan said. "I don't like it any more than you do, but those are military horns. The Bloodcloaks will be hunting for the murderers of their squads and I imagine the villagers would love to roast some mages. These witches are our best shot at survival."

Emma bristled. "Murderers? They *attacked us*, Declan. We were defending ourselves."

"You know that and I know that, deary. But they are religious zealots who know no reason. It is a fool's errand and suicide to try."

How do I know what the right choice is? What would her father do? He would fight, she was sure, as he was the bravest, or perhaps most foolish, man she knew. Perhaps it was better to ask what her *mother* would do. She was the pragmatic one. She would say "Live again to fight another day" or something to that effect. "All right, we'll go. Declan, take Charles again. Richard, do you know how to use that thing?" She gestured to the sword at his belt he had stolen from one of the Bloodcloaks.

"My dad and I used to spar."

"All right. Ethan, carry Alivia. Richard, be prepared to draw that thing." She turned a glare on Kylie as the men set about their assigned tasks. "Can you walk on your own?"

Kylie stepped back slightly under the weight of her glare. "Yes, I can."

"Good, because I'm in no mood to help someone who betrayed us." She stalked after the witches.

"Betrayed you?" Kylie asked, voice pained. "I just stood up for you with the grand matron!"

Emma whirled, heat rising in her cheeks. "A grand matron we knew *nothing about* until she showed up. It might have been something to tell us about *before* being ambushed by them!"

"In case you hadn't noticed, we were a little busy running from armed enemies." Now Kylie's eyes burned with anger while her jaw and fists clenched. "You could show a little gratitude."

Emma sniffed. "Let's go."

"Emma, we can't just leave the fire," Ethan said in a strained tone. He had just hoisted Alivia up into his arms and groaned under the strain.

She felt a moment of pity for him, but it wilted beneath the heat of her anger for Kylie. She refused to acknowledge the girl to ask for her help. Instead she walked near the fire and started kicking dirt on it. Not much happened at first.

Kylie remained where she was, arms crossed, watching. At last she sighed, in resignation or annoyance Emma couldn't tell, and spoke. "Do you want my help?"

"You'd probably just get us all burnt."

"Emma," Ethan scolded. "We don't have time for this bickering."

His words hit her like a slap in the face. She gave him a hurt expression but the sight of him straining to hold their teacher in his arms for a second time made her hold her tongue. At last she sighed. He was right, they didn't have time for this. And to be fair, she was being slightly childish. "Yes, please," she said, stepping away from the fire but not making eye contact with Kylie. Shame washed over her now.

Kylie stepped closer to the fire, stopping a few feet short of it, and raised her hand, palm toward the flame. Like with the dirt, nothing happened at first. Then the flame started to grow brighter, turning from reddish-orange to dark orange. The wood crackled and a whooshing sound erupted from the campfire. The sound increased until the pieces of wood were mere ash and the fire extinguished with a poof. The glade returned to being embraced only by the light of the moon high above.

The horns came again, closer this time. Kylie let out a deep breath. "We can go now."

Emma thought about thanking the girl, and even opened her mouth, but decided not to and snapped it shut. Instead she walked to the edge of the woods, searching for the path the witches had worn through the forest.

They walked in silence for a time, following the snapping of twigs and worn path through the undergrowth left by the witches. Emma had to stop several times at the insistence of the men because she was getting too far ahead of them. She stifled her annoyance that they were going too slow. Thrice more the horns came in the distance, each time seeming to be closer. She feared the Bloodcloaks, or worse, the villagers, would find them before they reached the coven.

Her fears were assuaged, however, as the path led to a cliff overlooking a river. A high waterfall fed what she thought must be the Silver River. "A dead end?" she asked Kylie, who came to stand beside her a moment later. Her anger at the girl had cooled like the night air after sunset and now she felt sheepish talking to her. She would have to apologize later, when they weren't running for their lives.

"No. Follow me," Kylie said, her face indiscernible in the moonlight but Emma thought she was smiling. She led them to a boulder nearby. Behind the boulder lay a path toward the water's edge. They trudged down the path, the grunts and groans of Ethan and Declan growing in frequency and volume as they went downhill, and came to the waterfall. Droplets splashed Emma's face like the water from the fountain in Trader's Square back in Ironforge. "In here." Kylie passed under the water and then disappeared *through* the waterfall.

Emma blinked. This was no time for a shower. What was the fool girl doing, drowning them? "Kylie?" she asked, not wanting to call out the foolishness of the girl...yet.

Kylie walked back through, clothes and hair drenched. "Come on. It's hollow behind the water."

"Oh," Emma said, dumbfounded. Of course. Her exhaustion must have been affecting her ability to think. As she stood there feeling foolish for the second, or was it the third, time that night her brother and the other two men passed through the waterfall. She took one more glance around, eyes alighting on the moon, before bracing herself and passing through the icy water. Inside, she found the others standing at the mouth of a long tunnel. A faint yellow light glowed in the distance enough to illuminate the walls.

Kylie led them down the tunnel in silence, the dripping of water off their clothes the only source of sound. The yellow light grew brighter and the warmth emanating from the stones below and around her increased with each step. They came to a bend in the tunnel and rounded it. Emma side-stepped to avoid running into her brother's back, then stared.

Spread out before them, in a vast subterranean cavern, stood dozens of stone structures adorned with torches and braziers. In the center of the cavern an enormous pyre burned, sending waves of heat toward them.

"Welcome to the coven," Kylie said with a smile.

Chapter 12

Along with heat, the coven radiated activity, like a hive of bees. Women and men scurried through makeshift streets between stone buildings, looking small from the high vantage point afforded to Emma.

A set of wide stone stairs led down into the cavern. Had the coven built this place?

"We don't know how this city came to be here," Kylie said, as if hearing her thoughts. "But our ancestors found this place centuries ago and have been here ever since. The waterfall provides our water and we hunt, gather or trade for food."

"Is that how you got caught? Trading in town for food?" Emma asked as they descended the stairs. The grand matron and the witches who had accompanied her earlier stood at the bottom awaiting them.

"Yes. I was sent in to town to trade jewelry for food. One of the dark mages must have sensed something and stopped me."

"You can sense another person's magic?"

Kylie shrugged. "I don't know of any other way they could have known I was a witch."

Perhaps a traitor in your midst? Emma wondered, but held her tongue and Kylie proved she could not, in fact, hear her thoughts, for she did not respond.

Ethan and Declan set their charges down on the stone floor of the ancient city. Declan stretched and rubbed his back. "Remind me to work out more or tell Charles to lose some weight." Even Ethan looked out of breath. Which Emma supposed was understandable given how many miles they had traveled.

"I am sure you are hungry, cold and tired," the grand matron said, a kind smile on her face and warmth in her eyes now that they were in a better lit environment. "We will prepare you a meal and warm bed for the evening. We can speak in the morning."

"And you're sure the Bloodcloaks won't find us?" As if summoned by her speaking their name, the sound of a horn echoed distantly down the hallway. It sounded different, though. Muffled, like it was under a blanket.

The grand matron's smile did not slip. "Child, our sisterhood has lived here in safety for over five hundred years. They shall not find us."

Her assurance mollified Emma slightly, but she couldn't help feeling like a cat trapped in a barrel.

Two pairs of men appeared as if summoned and carried Charles and Alivia toward a building ahead of the group on the left.

"Be careful with the black man," Emma called after them. "His name is Charles. He has an arrow in his back."

"We do have eyes," the grand matron reminded her, again. "He is in good hands here." She followed the men, most of the witches trailing after her.

The remaining four witches stepped forward. One led each member of Emma's group apart from Kylie to a building across from the one Charles and Alivia occupied. Kylie was led away into the streets of the city. Would they ever see the girl again? "Where is Kylie going?" she asked the plump witch guiding her.

"That need be none of your concern," the woman said.

"We saved her life and she saved us. I'm making her my concern." She tried to put steel into her voice like her mother had a knack for.

The woman rounded on her, exasperation evident on her face. "She is not your concern, child." She sighed when Emma replied with a glare. "Fine. She is going to report to the elders."

Report on what, us? "Will we get to meet these elders?"

"That is not up to me. Now may we go?" She said the last bit in a sarcastic tone and offered a mock curtsy.

Emma nodded, feeling abashed. She followed the plump woman into the square building, a building which looked like all the other square buildings. Inside she found wool rugs and two rows of wood-framed beds. A wash basin sat on a small table between every other bed while a fire burned in the hearth at the far end of the building sending forth waves of heat to welcome the newcomers. *Welcome to my domain*, the fire seemed to say as it crackled merrily.

"This is our guest house," one of the other women, a scrawny woman a head taller than Emma, said. "We do not receive many visitors, you are the first in many years."

"And the building across the way?"

"The medical building. There the grand matron and the others will tend to your friends."

"They're not our friends, exactly," Ethan said as he wandered by the hearth, holding out his hands. How he could be cold after carrying Alivia all this way baffled Emma.

Emma shot him a sharp look. What were they if not their friends? Yes, Alivia was an arch mage and supposed to be teaching them, but they could still consider her a friend, couldn't they?

"Your traveling companions, then," she replied, unperturbed.

"Can we get some grub?" Declan asked as he sat down on the bed. His face contorted, suggesting the mattress was not soft. Awfully refined tastes for a wagoner. "Food," he clarified in answer to the blank stare she gave him.

"Ah. We will bring you 'grub' momentarily."

Declan stretched and lay back on the bed. "It's not the Tower or the palace, but it will do."

How did a wagoner know what the beds in a palace were like? He had mentioned he was sometimes a bard. Emma opened her mouth to voice her thoughts when five men entered bearing plates of steaming food. Her stomach growled a greeting.

They served Richard first, who had finally re-sheathed his sword, though she didn't know why he hadn't done it when they first arrived at the coven. He sat silently on the side of his bed next to Emma. A heap of dark meat, quartered potatoes and a side of red berries occupied his plate. Steam rose from it. Had they known exactly when they would arrive? Or used magic to keep the food warm? There was so much she didn't know.

Declan was served next. He withdrew a knife from his sheath and flipped it into the air. He caught it with a swipe so deft Emma almost missed it and stabbed into the meat, ignoring the wooden spoon with its handle dangling over the side. He took a bite of the steaming meat and chewed. He closed his eyes and made an appreciative "mmmm" sound. "Ah, boar, tender and moist if I do say so myself."

"You do," Ethan said as he poked at the meat on his plate. "I don't like boar."

The plump witch smirked at his complaint. "I'm sure we could find some rat to make a stew. Would you prefer that?"

"Or are you a vegetarian?" Declan asked. "Strange people, vegetarians. Only eating plants as if they were sheep. You don't need to abstain from meat to prove yourself a sheep."

Emma didn't know anyone who only ate vegetables in Ironforge. Such a thing would have been commented upon. Perhaps they did things differently in Tar Ebon?

Ethan grumbled but ate the meat offered without further complaint. Their mother would have swatted him for complaining about free food offered in a desperate moment. Did he not understand the gravity of the situation they were in?

Emma received her plate and was about to hungrily dig in when the server placed another tray on the table next to her. "Who is that for?" she asked, fork halfway to her mouth.

As if summoned by her question, Kylie entered. She gave a small smile at seeing Emma, gave a curtsy to the witches and walked over to sit on the bed next to Emma. "Hello," she said, as if not sure how Emma would react.

Indeed, Emma was not sure how she was going to react. Yes, the girl had withheld information, but not out of malicious intent. In fact, she had saved them. Without her they would have wandered aimlessly in the woods until the Bloodcloaks caught them. They might have already been burning on the stake at that very moment, if they were allowed to survive that long. Then she remembered how awfully she had treated Kylie and the shame of the memory caused her to settle for "hello" in return instead of a more joyous response. She *was* happy to see Kylie. She had been worried the girl would be punished in some way. There were no bruises on her and she hadn't limped or winced as she walked over or sat down. She decided to ask anyway. "Did you get in trouble?"

The same five men re-appeared and gave out drinks to the five occupants of the house.

"Trouble?" Kylie asked. Behind her, the other witches were exiting. The plump one told them the wood for the fire was in a cabinet next to the hearth before closing the door behind her.

"With the elders. One of the witches said you were on your way to report to the council of elders."

"Oh. Yes. Well, first, we don't call ourselves 'witches.' We prefer the term 'sister' when referring to another magic-using woman."

"I'm sorry," Emma said, feeling abashed.

"But to answer your question, I did report to the council because my mother is on it. I wanted her to know I was safe."

"Oh." That made sense. No secret plans to betray them, nor floggings in what passed for the public square. Just reuniting with her mother. "And you chose to come back and spend the night here with us? Don't you have accommodations of your own?"

"Would you prefer I leave?" Kylie asked in a hurt voice. When Emma blanched she smiled and laughed. "I'm teasing. I do appreciate that you care about the comfort of my behind, though."

Emma couldn't help but laugh at that, even with a mouth full of potatoes. "They aren't the most comfortable," she agreed after swallowing her food.

"I returned because I didn't want you and your friends to be alone without a guide. I know how it is to be in a new place."

"You said you came here at ten," Emma said, recalling an earlier conversation. "How is it your mother is here also?"

"The sisters here go out into the world for a time. They meet a man, have a child and raise the child there. They continue having children until they have a girl. Then when their first girl turns ten, if they manifest magic, the mother and child come here, to the coven, along with their family."

"Oh, so you didn't abandon your family."

Kylie looked horrified at the thought. "Of course not! But this way the coven doesn't have to exile families who have no magical children. If a sister has no children, no girls or no girls with the power of magic they do not return."

"That part is sad."

"It is necessary for the survival of the coven." That part sounded rehearsed, as if it were recited by rote. "Without such a mechanism the coven would grow beyond its ability to sustain itself and draw too much attention."

Attention from who? "Do women ever refuse to leave? Or try to come back when they have no daughters with magic in tow?"

"Rarely. It is against our customs and forbidden, but there have been some. One woman a year or two ago, named Esmeralda, returned barren and a widow. An exception was made for her but..." she lowered her voice, "...it was later learned she'd killed her children *and* her husband."

Emma's eyes went wide with shock. "She murdered her entire family? I take it none had magic?"

"Correct. None of the children had magic, so she found them impure and killed them. Once the elders found out they exiled her. She didn't want to go, and fought them, but in the end she lost and fled."

Such drama for a coven. To be fair, they had brought it on themselves, Emma thought. "My father told me about the druids of the forest. They did something similar, exiling certain druids every generation as required by a prophecy. My father said sometimes people do things not because they are rational but because they are customary."

"Do you disagree with our customs?" Kylie asked in a neutral tone as she took a bite of boar.

"No, as I don't know much about them in full and am not part of your culture. I was just trying to see the other side of things." She decided a change of subject was in order. "Did you hear anything about Alivia or Charles before you entered?"

Kylie too seemed relieved for a change in the conversation. "I heard nothing, but the grand matron had not yet emerged. I am sure we'll hear something by morning. We should get some sleep, though."

Emma rubbed her eyes and exhaustion hit her in a wave. She nodded in agreement, laid down and fell asleep.

Chapter 13

Emma awoke. The fire had burned to embers while they slept, though Ethan now knelt by it, feeding it wood. Kylie and the others still slumbered. Being underground, it was impossible to tell what time it was looking through the windows of the building, but a time piece on the wall told her it was early morning. She slipped out of bed and padded toward her brother. She wore the same clothing as the day before - the horrible day. A day she wished she could forget.

"Keeping the fire alive?" she asked, not knowing what else to say, which was silly since this was her brother. She should be able to talk to her own brother, shouldn't she? Why now were things awkward?

He looked up and then back down to the wood in his hands before tossing another log in. "Yeah, I guess." He sounded sullen, hopeless.

"We didn't really get to talk much more about yesterday," she began. "Did you want to talk?"

Ethan didn't turn around or speak.

She waited a few moments then, "Ethan? What's wrong?"

"I already told you. And you blew me off."

"Ethan..." How did she go about explaining? "I'm sorry." That was a start, right? "We were running for our lives. In the heat of the moment I may have been impatient."

"Yeah. I may have snapped a little too."

A little? You almost bit my head off, she thought, but decided against saying that. "Can we put yesterday behind us? We're the only family we have out here. And remember what Mom and Dad said about family."

Ethan stood. She embraced him and he awkwardly returned the gesture. They hadn't been ones to hug as children. Usually they fought, with him picking on her and calling her a snitch if she told their parents. She smiled at the memory. Oh to be children again.

A sense of movement from behind caused Emma to turn. Kylie was rising and stretching. She met Emma's eyes and smiled. Emma smiled in return. "Do you need any more help with the fire?" she asked.

"Nah, I got it. Go see your new girlfriend." He rolled his eyes and went back to chucking wood into the fireplace.

Girlfriend? She supposed they were friends after talking last night, but she didn't think of Kylie in a romantic sense. Granted, she didn't think of a muscular man like Richard as attractive either. She hadn't found her "type" yet. She strode over to Kylie, smile fading a little in response to her brother's words. Maybe she was giving the wrong message with a broad smile? Why did life have to be so complicated? "Good morning," she said.

Kylie's smile had not lost its brightness. "Good morning. How long have you been up?"

"Only a few minutes. Ethan took care of the fire."

"I see that." She paused and a silence stretched between them that approached awkwardness. "Do you want to visit Alivia and Charles?"

Emma nodded. "Yes, I would like that. We're going across the street," she called to Ethan. "You'll tell the others?"

Her brother waved in acknowledgment before plopping back down on the straw mattress. She had to admit not remembering much after her head hit the bed. The straw hadn't bothered her as much as she thought it would.

Kylie led Emma out of the guest house. Witches - sisters, she reminded herself firmly - were already up and about, going who knew where in the fire-light gloom. What did all these women do for vocations? Did they have money, or was it a barter system? Who went out and got the food and who cooked it? Questions upon questions whirled in Emma's head, begging to be asked, but she focused instead on the door they approached - the door to the infirmary.

The inside of the medical building resembled the guest house almost exactly. An identical hearth burned at one end and two rows of six beds each lined the walls of the building. One difference was torches occupying the space between beds, casting additional light and sending out more heat. Emma's eyes fell on the only two occupants of the building.

Alivia had been taken out of her dress and now wore a worn shift. Charles wore what looked like a rucksack bag but was probably baggy trousers and a tunic. Two sisters shared the building with the unconscious individuals. One such was the grand matron herself, sitting beside Alivia's bed. She studied them as they approached. "Ah, did you get rest, child?"

Emma nodded. "Yes, thank you."

"We will have to do something about your clothes. Several of the sisters set about sewing new outfits yesterday. They should be done soon."

"That would be welcome," Emma said. She gestured to Alivia. "Has there been any change?"

"In the woman? Alivia you said her name was, yes? We have fed her broth and water to help build her strength. Still she remains unconscious."

"Is that normal?" Fear lodged in Emma's gut. What if Alivia's brain was damaged and she would never wake? She'd heard tales of that happening to men at the forges or in the mines when heavy objects met their skulls. "She will awaken, yes?"

The grand matron nodded. "We have delved her body and believe her brain is intact. She simply needs more rest. How did she come to be in this state?"

"She cast lightning twice on two groups of Bloodcloaks. After commanding the flames to cease burning around Kylie."

"Yes, that would drain her strength. Even one of those tasks would put any sister of ours in such a state. I am impressed she managed three in a brief time."

"And him?" she asked, pointing to Charles. The plump woman from the night before sat there. She nodded to Emma but looked to the grand matron.

"The arrow was removed, but he lost a great deal of blood. An infection was beginning but we purged it and gave him herbs to continue warding it away."

Emma sighed in relief. "Kylie said you possessed healing magic. So he will make a full recovery?"

"In time, yes. He is still weak and needs rest, but he no longer has a hole in his back." This was evidenced by Charles laying on his back now.

"How long for him?" Her mind drifted to their original quest - to reach the steam wagon and arrive at Tar Ebon to train. Would the steam wagon remain indefinitely? Or had the Bloodcloaks gotten to it or driven it away? Thinking of the Bloodcloaks, where were they? Would they find the coven? Or would they give up and move on to easier prey? The thought of the Bloodcloaks "moving on" frightened her more than them finding the coven. At least the sisters could defend themselves, right?

The grand matron shrugged. "Could be hours, could be days. We cannot know these things. But I see the worry in your eyes, child. You worry about the Bloodcloaks?"

"How could you tell?" Although she knew the sisters could not read minds as she'd tested it with Kylie, she still narrowed her eyes. Was her face that transparent?

"Because many of the sisters here are expressing similar concerns about the so-called Shield of Man. Such a deceitful name."

"I suppose I am a bit worried," she lied. Terrified was more like it, after hearing the other sisters were worried too.

"Our coven has existed undetected for centuries, child. A few bigots will not change that."

"What of the reports of dark mages?"

"Having magic does not mean they can see through the earth. Unless they know where we are they will be as disadvantaged as the Bloodcloaks."

"I see." That did make her feel a little better.

"I have an idea to help take your mind off the troubles of the world. I want you to begin training with your magic."

"You want me to become a sister of the coven?" she asked cautiously. *She didn't want that, did she?*

The grand matron smirked. "Don't seem so horrified at the thought, child." She held up a hand to forestall any protestations from Emma. "You can continue on your way to become a mage," she waved a hand toward Alivia. "I would not deny you that. But, we are not much different from the mages of Tar Ebon. We all manipulate the elements of existence."

"Then why didn't the coven come out of hiding and join the Tower?"

The grand matron smiled sadly. "We were given a quest, my dear. A task that can only be carried out in this place. Ours is the role of guardian."

"Guardian of what?" Her curiosity was piqued now, and it seemed even Kylie's interest had been kindled.

"A tale for another time I am afraid. What say you? Will you let us instruct you for a time?"

Yes, she thought. *Yes, yes, yes, of course.* But the faces of Richard and Ethan intruded on her thoughts. "What about Richard and Ethan? They are mages in training also. Can they be instructed?"

The grand matron pursed her lips, though she nodded sagely as if she had expected the request. "It is unusual, but I do not think the council will reject the request. We will allow them to participate in the training sessions. Does that satisfy you?"

"Yes." She could picture Ethan's face if she'd told him she was being trained and not him.

The grand matron clapped her hands. "Excellent. Return to your building and wait. I will send someone to bring you and your companions clean clothing, breakfast and a wash basin." She then turned her attention back to Alivia, signaling the discussion was over.

Emma curtsied anyway, murmured her thanks and left the building, Kylie at her side.

Once outside, Kylie took Emma's hand to halt her. "I'm sorry I didn't speak much in there." She tipped her head toward the building. "She intimidates me."

"It's all right," Emma assured her. "There were no arguments for you to intervene in. Come on, my stomach is growling and I feel dirty."

They entered the guest housing and found that Declan and Richard were now up. Breakfast had been brought already, as had clothing. A large wash tub sat by the hearth and small buckets occupied the tables nearest their beds. It looks like the sisters were ahead of their grand matron on the hospitality part.

"Ah, the errant mage returns!" Declan exclaimed. "How fares our valiant leaders?"

"Charles has been healed but hasn't awoken yet, Alivia is much the same as before."

"Ah, a pity," Declan said. "We could use their guidance about now."

Emma bristled at that. "We are in good hands here."

"You mean women are in good hands here. Us men, well, I swear the 'sisters' who brought us our breakfast looked at us like we were pieces of meat being sized up by a butcher. Though I suppose the corpse of a cow is also in 'good hands' when a butcher has ahold of it."

"You are free to leave if you wish," Kylie chimed in. "No one is stopping you."

Declan raised an eyebrow at her. "I am tempted to take you up on that offer, my dear, but these children," his gesture included Ethan, Richard and, to Emma's chagrin, her, "need guidance and support from an older," he puffed up his chest, "more dignified person."

Emma rolled her eyes. "We're going to be training with the sisters. All of us with magic," she clarified upon seeing Ethan's surprise. Richard continued eating his food, watching her but making no gesture of surprise, happiness or anger. It was hard to read the boy. "They manipulate the elements the same way we do, so while we wait for Alivia and Charles to awaken we are going to train."

"Was this your idea?" Declan asked. "Or the grand matron?"

"It was her idea, but I agreed to it and it makes sense, does it not?"

"When traveling through the desert a man is wise to not stop for too long at an oasis."

"Why is that? An oasis has water and shade."

"Because predators are attracted by those same things. Especially at night."

"Speak plainly, wagoner." *If he's even a wagoner.* "Are you saying the sisters are dangerous?"

"Oh no, they are like the sweet coolness of the water in a desert, my dear. But I would beware tarrying too long lest predators find us."

"The Bloodcloaks, you mean?"

"Or others. You said there were dark mages out there too, yes? Nasty folks."

"How does a wagoner know about dark mages and whether they are nasty or not?" Emma challenged him.

"They are called 'dark' for a reason, my dear. It is not a stretch to assume they're evil."

Emma narrowed her eyes. There was more to his original statement than he was letting on. He was deflecting. She considered pressing him but stopped. Now was not the time. Her stomach seconded that decision, glad for the arguing to be done. "Thank you for your wise counsel," was all she said before focusing on eating. Minutes later she washed her face and exposed skin in the wash basin, then grabbed the faded clothing she'd been offered and went to a room behind the guest house where she could dress.

"Did Emma get replaced with a sack of potatoes?" Ethan asked dryly upon seeing her new outfit. She carried her old clothes in her arms.

For the first time that day Richard made a noise. He laughed out loud.

Emma shot them both a glare, then looked at their own clothing. "Your stuff isn't much better." Indeed, while she wore a faded gray dress her male companions had been offered brown tunics and trousers so faded they almost looked gray themselves. "I thought the grand matron said sisters were working since last night on new clothing." That sentence she directed to Kylie, who blushed.

"The grand matron may have misspoken. They did indeed sew new clothing, but not for you and your companions. Rather, the new clothing was for the men and women your clothing was obtained from."

"The royal treatment," Declan said with a smirk. As if he knew anything about how royals were treated.

"Well, I for one was glad to change out of my old clothes, regardless of what they're replaced with."

"Don't worry, your old clothing will be returned once they're washed and repaired if necessary."

"See?" she challenged Ethan.

He held up his hands as if to profess his innocence. "Excuse me while I go change." He rose and went to the back room to change, skipping the wash basin.

A SHORT WHILE LATER, after everyone was changed, washed and fed, the four companions and Kylie stood in an open patch of rock near the center of the coven. A statue of an unknown woman occupied the center of the square. In front of them stood Sister Griswold. She clapped her hands. "Now, who can see the magic I just performed?" she asked.

Ethan and Kylie raised their hands. Emma shot a jealous glance toward her brother. Meanwhile *she* was still unable to see how Sister Griswold performed a manipulation of the stone block in front of her. The center of the stone had retracted as if being drilled and it now sported a hole clean through.

"Emma and Richard. You must concentrate."

Easy for her to say, Emma thought. She was trying, truly she was. She closed her eyes and tried to feel...something...at the edge of her awareness.

"I will demonstrate again. Watch not with your eyes, listen not with your ears, but with your *mind*." She began using magic, though she would not tell them what object was the target or what she was doing to it. That was left to them, the students, to determine and answer.

She felt a vibration beneath her feet, a shaking of the ground. Her eyes wanted to open, to *look* at the ground, but she forced them shut. Her ears wanted to listen to the ground, perhaps for a distant rumbling. She shut that sense off too. Silence. In its place she somehow stretched her mind toward the vibration her feet felt. There, she could "see" in her mind's eye the dirt. It vibrated faster than the ground around it. What was the purpose of that? Then the ground softened beneath her feet. She screeched and leapt away before her feet were swallowed.

Sister Griswold opened her eyes and smiled. "Good! You could sense the softening of the earth, couldn't you?"

Emma nodded. "Yes. You made it vibrate faster, which made it less firm."

She nodded. "Correct. Richard, did you sense anything?"

He shook his head and hung his head in shame.

Sister Griswold frowned and made a tut sound. "Typical man."

Anger rose in Emma and she opened her mouth to say something but closed it at a sharp glance from her instructor.

"Do you have something to say, Emma? Does your friend need a defender?"

Emma held her gaze for several seconds while she debated saying something regardless of the consequences, then looked away. When she looked at Richard he was watching her, a slight smile on his face. "No, of course not."

"A wise decision." She continued droning on about sensing and manipulating the elements of existence or "elements" for short and Emma tried to pay attention. But the anger bubbling beneath the surface threatened to derail her concentration.

She had them practice sensing manipulation of the elements several more times. On the fifth try Richard said he could sense her manipulation of the wind. She gave him grudging praise in response.

They had yet to practice manipulating the elements themselves yet. But the day passed into afternoon and their instructor gave them a break for the rest of the day. "Tomorrow we will continue practicing sensing. Then, as I'm sure some of you are wondering," her eyes fell on Emma in particular, "we will begin learning how to manipulate the elements once I feel you can sufficiently sense what you are manipulating."

The boys returned to the guest house while Kylie offered to give Emma a tour of the coven. They traveled the perimeter of the coven, which was much smaller than Emma originally thought. When she asked how many sisters lived at the coven Kylie told her it fluctuated around seventy, including mundane husbands or children. *So few*, Emma thought. *And all for what?* The insinuation by the grand matron that they had been charged with something, such as defending something, continued to nag at her. She didn't bother asking Kylie, for she had seen the same look of ignorance on the girl's face. Clearly it was important if generations of women had sacrificed their lives to live beneath the earth.

The two girls passed through the square their training had taken place in earlier and she asked, "Who is that statue of?"

"That is the statue of our founder, Lady Magdalen."

The founder? Surely she knew their purpose. She would have given them their purpose. "Did she find this place alone?"

"No. It began with fifty men and fifty women, all capable of magic."

"Men too?" A memory of the day before surfaced. "What happened to the men?"

"They went mad with power. They sought to control something that was beyond them. A civil war erupted and the men were all killed or driven out."

"And that something is what the coven protects, isn't it? You truly don't know what it is?" Now that they were on the topic Emma felt more confident pressing her for information.

Kylie shook her head. "No. We are not taught what the artifact is, only that its importance is paramount to the safety of this world."

"And the men threatened that safety?"

"That is what the legend says." She looked around, as if looking for listening ears. "Between you and me, the entrance to the vault is below the council building. A secret entrance my mother told me about when she was too far in her cups. She doesn't remember telling me, so promise you won't tell anyone."

"I promise, I won't."

"What do you think of Richard?" she asked, clearly wanting to change the subject.

Emma blinked. "I think he's all right. A little too manly for my tastes."

"*Too* manly? What continent are you from?"

"Ha. Very funny. Why, do you like him?"

Kylie blushed. "I think he's kind of cute. And I like his humble shyness."

"Being quiet can also be a form of arrogance. If one thinks they're better than everyone else."

"I think I can tell the difference. There are some extremely arrogant sisters here who I can't stand. He's nothing like them."

"Then what are you doing standing here with me? Go talk to him." Emma gave the girl a shove and she giggled.

"It's not that easy. There are expectations here."

"What sort of expectations?"

"Like not...having relations..." her cheeks burned. "...until we're ready to commit to marriage."

Emma screwed her face up in distaste. "That seems counterproductive. How do you know if the person you're settling down with is a good guy if you can't compare him to anyone else?" As she said it she remembered that it was similar in Ironforge. At least for women. Men could carouse, albeit in secret, all the time, but young women were expected to remain chaste until marriage. Her mother told her once she agreed with the sentiment of no sex until marriage but didn't agree with the way they only held the women to the same standard. She called it "sexist."

Kylie shrugged. "It's just the way it is, I guess."

They walked in silence the remainder of the way to the guest house.

Chapter 14

The next morning Alivia was in the same condition but, to Emma's delight, Charles was awake. And he was not happy.

"Get away from me!" he screamed, scooting back in the bed, eyes wild. Emma witnessed this the instant she walked in the medical building.

Three sisters stood by, trying to calm him down. The grand matron remained by Alivia but watched the drama unfold with an amused smile. Kylie had gone to visit her mother and Emma wished she was there right then.

Emma approached Charles. "Charles, it's me, Emma." She waved her hands, attempting to get his attention. "You're safe."

At first her words had no effect on the man, for he continued to scream and swat away any hands belonging to sisters trying to help him. When she repeated herself his eyes focused on her and he said, "Emma, is that you?"

"Yes, it's me." She took a step toward him. "You're safe, you're safe."

His eyes darted between the three sisters, suspicion heavy in them. "Who are these women?"

"They're...sisters of a coven." She raised her hand when his eyes opened wide. "But they have magic like us. They won't hurt us."

"How do I know you're real?" Charles challenged. "This could be a trick. Emma could be dead!"

Emma's shoulders sagged in frustration. Why was he this distrustful? Had his mind been damaged by the injury? Or did he have some experience with covens of women? "Ask me something only I would know." That was admittedly very little considering they had only met in Ironforge.

"What is your father's name?" he asked.

"Jeremy," Emma replied without hesitation.

"Wrong!" Charles crowed. "Wrong, wrong, wrong!" He held his head in his hands and rocked back and forth.

Emma looked to the grand matron and pleaded with her eyes. What was wrong with the man?

She rose from her seat and strode over. "It is possible his mind was wounded during the fighting, either from a blow or infection from the wound spreading to it."

Emma had never heard of infections in the brain. She'd seen insane people over the years, though. But Charles hadn't been insane before he woke up. "What can we do to help him?" She stopped, sensing something. She closed her eyes and sensed Charles reaching out to the walls with his magic. The elements within the wall vibrated. Was he trying to bring down the building?

The grand matron must have had the same thought, for Emma sensed her reaching out with her own magic to combat Charles' magic. The stone nearest Charles' bed softened and solidified, back-and-forth. Then Charles gave up on that and summoned fire, drawing the heat from the room - Emma saw the waves of heat swirling toward a space above his hand. She braced herself to intercept the flames if he attacked her or the grand matron.

"Stop!" Alivia shouted.

Emma spun around and gaped. Alivia walked forward from her bed. She passed the grand matron, eyes never leaving Charles. The flows of magic had stopped, though the flame persisted, as Charles' eyes opened in surprise. "Alivia?" he asked.

"Stop this foolishness, Charles. Remember who you are and why you're here."

He shook, visibly trying to do something. Was he trying to do what Alivia asked? Or was he about to go into another fit of rage? Her question was answered a moment later when the flame in his hand dissipated, sending waves of heat cascading through the room and washing over Emma, and he let out a sob. "Oh, Alivia, I am so sorry."

"Don't apologize to me," Alivia said, words like steel. "You almost attacked these poor women. You owe *them* the apology."

The grand matron shook her head. "That won't be necessary." She smiled kindly at Charles - a reaction Emma hadn't expected. She'd expected her face to be a mask of fury, much like what she saw on the other three sisters, not forgiveness. "No one was hurt and I understand the instinct to defend oneself in an unknown situation. He was merely confused."

Charles bowed his head. "Thank you." He looked back to Emma. "Emma, I...am sorry I didn't believe you. I..." his eyes flicked to Alivia and back, "...wasn't in my right mind."

"I figured you weren't, considering the fact you wanted to bring the building down and burn us." Emma smirked to take the sting out of her comment. She pointed at Alivia. "How did you wake up?"

Alivia raised an eyebrow. "Did you expect me to never wake up?"

Emma blushed. "No. It's just...," she struggled to express herself. "We were worried about you and didn't know how long it would be for you to wake up." The last sentence came out in a rush.

The arch mage smiled. "I'm glad you cared for my well-being. Where are we and how long was I unconscious?"

"We're in a coven of sisters. They found us after we escaped from the town. You've been unconscious for two days now."

"I've seen longer periods of unconsciousness after magical exertion. You can tell me more later." She bowed her head to the grand matron. "Thank you for taking care of both me and my students and Charles."

"Of course," the grand matron bowed her head in return.

"You have magic? I sensed you and Charles dueling."

"Yes. We...use the same magic as your order of mages," she replied.

Alivia's eyes ranged over the other sisters still crowded around Charles' bed. "Well, perhaps we can discuss more over dinner. But I for one am famished." Her smile seemed forced now.

"Emma can lead you both to the guest building. We will fetch you shortly to dine together," the grand matron said. She gestured to the door of the medical building and Emma took her cue, walking slowly toward the door so that Charles and Alivia could follow. She felt the eyes of the sisters on her back.

As they entered the guest house the men rose in shock. "Welcome to our humble abode," Declan said, bowing and motioning Alivia and Charles inside.

Ethan locked eyes with Emma. "Did you wake them up?" he asked her.

"No, I had nothing to do with it. Charles woke up before I got there and Alivia woke up while he was..." she stopped, not wanting to embarrass the arch mage.

"Confused," Alivia finished for her. "Charles was confused, and with good reason." She looked to Emma. "Tell me what happened."

Ten minutes later Emma concluded with, "...and the witches, I mean sisters, led us here. We couldn't leave without you and Charles and couldn't take you with us in the states you were in. The Bloodcloaks would have gotten us if we'd stayed out there. We didn't have a choice." She felt defensive, though Alivia had made a handful of comments for clarification but no rebukes.

"You did well," she replied. She glanced around the stone building. "A hidden city. I'd heard rumors of this place, you know? The archives tell of families disappearing and a general absence of magical candidates from this region. I never gave the reports much credence. You said they're protecting something?"

"Yes, they said it was a task given to them or..." she halted when the door opened and Kylie entered. "Alivia, this is my friend and guide, Kylie. She's the girl you rescued."

Kylie gaped at Alivia - at her savior. "I...um...I wanted to thank you, Arch Mage, for protecting me. You saved my life." She offered an awkward curtsy.

"Rise, child," Alivia responded, a kindly smile plastered on her face. "I would have protected anyone about to be burned in that moment. I am glad it was you." She glanced between Emma and Kylie. "Do the two of you need a moment?"

"No," Kylie squeaked, not looking at Emma. "I'm here to escort all of you to the dining hall."

"Oooh, there's a dining hall," Declan declared. "Fancy. I wonder if they need a bard."

Emma didn't particularly relish the idea of hearing any music the wagoner might make or stories he might tell. Though she did want to know how he thought he knew what being in a palace was like. Perhaps he'd delivered wine to one in the past?

"There won't be time for merriment," Alivia said. "We're eating and leaving."

"Wait, we're leaving?" Emma asked. "But they were..." the words died in her throat.

"They were what?" Alivia's eyes bored into her soul.

"They were training us in the ways of magic," she finished in a near-whisper.

She sniffed. "All the more reason to leave. I don't want you corrupted by their influence." She snapped a finger at Kylie when the girl opened her mouth to speak. "Not a word out of you. It's nothing personal, but we need to be moving on as fast as possible. The presence of so many Bloodcloaks worries me."

Emma cleared her throat. She'd forgotten to mention this part. "There are more than just Bloodcloaks out there. Kylie said it was dark mages who captured her."

Alivia's eyes narrowed. "Cultists, no doubt. Then that settles it. We're leaving now. Gather your things," she ordered.

"What about dinner?" Ethan blurted.

"We don't have time to sit around eating and drinking while bloody dark mages are searching for us."

"The grand matron said we were safe here. She said the dark mages couldn't sense beneath the earth or find us."

"If the Cult of Rae are here they're here for a reason. They were...defeated...eighteen years ago. They wouldn't risk coming out of hiding if it weren't important. They are not to be underestimated." She pointed to their beds. "Pack your things." She spun to Kylie, who was backing toward the door. "Girl, where are mine and Charles' things?"

Kylie shuddered with fear or indecision, Emma couldn't decipher which. "They're...," she pointed behind her toward the medical building. "But you can't...leave."

"And are you going to stop us?" Her tone suggested that would be a severe mistake.

Kylie shook her head fervently.

"Good. Gather your things," she said to the others. "We'll get our stuff on the way out. Not that we have much left to us since *you* lost the carriage," she directed the last sentence to Declan.

He held up his hands to profess his innocence. "Hoodlums, I tell you. They stole the carriage during the bedlam of the battle."

"You had one job, Declan, one job." She gave him a stern look that lasted only a handful of seconds before morphing into a smile. "And you did it. Thank you for keeping these three alive."

Declan bowed. "Of course, m'lady."

Emma stood there gaping for a moment, wondering what history Alivia and Declan had together, when she realized she wasn't packing. She went to her bunk and packed what meager possessions she owned into her belt satchel.

Kylie, who surprisingly hadn't fled, came to sit next to her on the bed. "You could stay here with us. With me."

"Funny, I was going to say you could come with us." Emma sighed, looked around aimlessly and gestured. "What kind of life is this for you? Don't you want to be free to roam the world?"

"Free in service of the Tower?" she asked. "Free to serve the mundanes while sleeping in a prison shaped like a tower?"

Emma stared at her in surprise. How could she talk like this? Service to anyone was a joy, her father had taught her that. Kylie acted like she was better than non-magical people. And to say the Tower was a prison? What was she on about? Had she been brain-washed by the sisterhood that much? "I would rather go out into the world and serve *all* people, even if that means giving up some of my freedoms, than sit here hiding the Founders-know-what."

Kylie's head snapped back as though she'd been slapped. "I'll have you know," she began, raising her voice, "I asked my mother what it was beneath the village. What it was we're defending. Ask her," she jerked her head toward Alivia, "about the Staff of Agamar."

Alivia's head whipped around, for Kylie had spoken it loud enough to be heard. She strode over, eyes locked on the blonde-haired girl. "What did you just say?"

"You heard me," Kylie challenged, the fear and indecision she'd shown earlier washed away by bravado. "We guard the Staff of Agamar."

"No," Alivia said. "You serve the Staff of Agamar." She turned to Charles. "That is why you awoke in such a state. You sensed the staff and didn't know it."

"And why there are no male mages here," Charles agreed. "All the better that we leave at once. Best to be away from that evil."

"It's not evil!" Kylie shouted, jumping to her feet. "The staff is the instrument of our salvation. The prophecies say when the demons come the staff shall set men free."

"By destroying them," Alivia said through gritted teeth. "Everyone out, now!" she froze, eyes staring toward the ceiling. "Oh no, it's too late." A second later a horn blast echoed through the window. It was coming from *inside* the village. A Bloodcloak horn. The building shook.

Charles and Alivia were the first out, then Declan, Richard with his sword out and Ethan and Emma. Kylie brought up the rear. Emma resisted the urge to shove her back in the building or punch her in the face. They didn't have time for that, however.

She looked up toward the point where the tunnel from the waterfall emptied into the cave that housed the village. Dozens of Bloodcloaks stood there, bows out and arrows knocked. To their flanks stood men and women of varying heights wearing black cloaks. The dark mages, Emma guessed. A throng of villagers descending the ramp into the heart of the village drew her attention away and prevented her from studying them further. The villagers spread out once they were on ground level and ran in-between the buildings and into them. Screams of surprise wafted from the windows of various buildings, followed by cries of pain and shouts of anger.

"We are attacked!" the grant matron's voice came from Emma's right. It boomed louder than it had before, suggesting she was amplifying it.

Way to state the obvious, Emma thought. As if the horns hadn't been enough.

As if on cue, as if they had been waiting to be acknowledged before attacking, the archers raised their bows and fired. Arrows soared through the air. One struck a fleeing man in the back, while a woman holding the hand of two children was shot through the neck. The arrows that descended on Emma's group were burned to ash by Charles or Alivia - Emma couldn't tell which because her concentration was so broken.

Behind the Bloodcloak line a familiar man sat atop a horse. Rahman, the commander of the Bloodcloaks, had ridden a horse into the cavern. He bellowed words made unintelligible due to the distance and pointed.

"Is there a back way out?" Alivia demanded of Kylie. The girl stared at her, a vacant expression on her face. "Girl! Is there a back way out?" Again she was met with vacancy. She slapped Kylie, which caused her to shake her head.

"What?"

"A back entrance. A way out. Where is it? Surely you have one."

The girl hesitated. Did she not know or was she deciding whether to help them? Emma touched her elbow. "Please, Kylie."

"Can you hurry it up," Declan said. "We've got company." Indeed, a group of ten villagers approached, holding rusty iron weapons and wooden clubs. Enough to kill them if given enough time. Between the arrows and the villagers they were running out of time. Declan removed two daggers from his belt and parried a sword blow while Richard swung his sword and sliced a man open at the gut. Ethan grabbed the club from the wounded man and parried a pitchfork thrust. Charles hung back, obviously protecting against further arrow strikes.

"I can't leave my mother alone," Kylie protested. Tears welled up in her eyes.

Emma wanted to say she didn't care about Kylie's mother. She wanted to lash out and say she didn't care about Kylie either. But she stopped and took a breath. All lives were precious and valuable. She smiled. And, as her father said, you got more bees with honey. "If we help rescue your mother will you show us the way out?" She met Alivia's eyes and received a small nod of approval.

Kylie met Emma's eyes and nodded. "Yes, I will."

"Lead the way."

"Wait!" Alivia said. She rushed into the medical building, emerging seconds later with the pouches belonging to her and Charles and a strange necklace she put on. "Okay, go."

Kylie led the group toward the center of town where the council building was. Women and men rushed not toward the rear of the cavern but toward the villagers and bowmen. One sister along their path hurled fire toward the ridge. It splashed into several archers and they fell screaming to the ground below. A second ball of flame was deflected, however, and a moment later the sister fell screaming to the ground, clutching at her head as her skin melted. The dark mages had entered the battle.

Screaming villagers chased after them. Charles stopped at one point and held his hand palm-out toward them. They stopped as if hitting an invisible wall, their noses pressed up against the barrier. He maintained it until all of them had crashed into it before running to catch up with the group.

The statue at the center loomed ahead. The grand matron and several witches, Emma had no qualms calling them that now, formed a circle around it. Lines were drawn in the sand between each witch and the statue. A summoning ritual? Her unspoken question was answered a moment later when they began chanting in an unknown language. Emma stopped against her will, eyes transfixed on the scene. The staff in the right hand of the female statue glowed a bright yellow. "The staff," Emma whispered. "The staff!" she shouted louder when none of the others noticed. She pointed toward the statue. "It's glowing. That staff is glowing!"

"Don't look at it!" Alivia shouted. "Don't touch it. Keep moving!" The building housing the council of elders loomed ahead.

Emma reluctantly followed the group, though she felt a heavy weight on her mind telling her to turn back. Her legs and arms felt weak, as if she were pulling a wagon. Still she continued. Kylie passed the council chambers and picked up her pace. Where was she taking them? She led them to the edge of the underground city.

The screams of witches and their husbands and children mingling with the cries of rage from the villagers continued to echo. The air felt colder, so cold in fact clouds blew from her mouth as she rushed to keep up. The ceiling of the cavern began to shake. They wouldn't bring the whole cavern down, would they? She didn't know what their goal was.

At the edge of the coven sat a small stone building. Kylie knocked on it frantically. "Mother, Mother!" She opened the door and rushed inside.

Emma took that moment to look back at the carnage. They'd lost the trail of angry mob and were out of range of the arrows. The witches and dark mages continued to exchange blows with fire, lightning and ice while the Bloodcloak archers looked to have been mostly decimated. Her mind drifted back to the glowing staff. "What about the staff? Is that what the dark mages are after?" she asked. She meant the question for Alivia, but Charles answered.

"She has a point, Alivia."

"We have more important things to worry about. Like getting out of here alive."

Charles continued to look at her, silent.

She groaned in annoyance. "Don't look at me like that."

"You know what has to be done. I'll do it alone if I have to."

Alivia shook her head. "No, we're in this fight together." She focused on Emma and took her necklace off. A locket hung from it. "Emma, I'm entrusting this to you."

Emma swallowed. It seemed like Alivia was saying goodbye. As if she were planning to sacrifice herself. "Alivia, I can't...you need it."

"You can give it back to me when we meet again." She smiled sadly.

"Why do I get the feeling we won't meet again?" Emma challenged.

Alivia looked to where the top of the statue holding the staff was visible over the stone buildings. Then she looked to the ceiling. "Because there's a chance we may not. Whatever happens you *must* reach the Tower. The steam wagon is the fastest way, and this amulet will get you passage on it. If that way is blocked, use whatever means available to reach Tar Ebon. Do you understand?"

"Yes," Emma said, tears welling up.

The door to the building opened and Kylie emerged with her mother, a gray-haired woman with a middle-aged face. "We're ready."

Alivia ignored the girl and turned to Declan. "Take care of them, you old fool."

Declan bowed with a flourish. "I shall endeavor to do so, m'lady. Though I would not be so sure of your mortality this day."

"We all must die."

"Most of us," Declan corrected.

"*All* of us," she countered. "Just some sooner than others." She blew him a kiss and started walking toward the center of the coven, Charles at her side.

Emma watched them go until a cough from Ethan made her turn around and blink. Everyone watched her. She cleared her throat. "You heard her. Let's get going. Where is the back door out of here?"

"Follow me," Kylie's mother said. She led them toward the rock wall furthest from the entrance. There the rock tapered to a point. "Only the elders know of this, and the rest are occupied," she jerked her head toward the fighting. She pressed her hand to the rock and it melted into the ground. Beyond lay a tunnel stretching upward into the darkness. She and Kylie entered, followed by the men and with Emma bringing up the rear. She paused and looked back. The ceiling was shaking more now and large chunks of rock were beginning to fall. A bright light shone from the center and then was extinguished. A whirlwind rose toward the roof of the cavern and rocks started falling in a torrent. The dust blocked her view and she hurried into the tunnel. A loud crash sounded behind her and she imagined the entire cavern caving in.

They walked for an indeterminate amount of time, their path lit by a flame glowing in Kylie's mother's hand, before coming to another wall. She again put her hand to it and it melted away. They emerged into a grassy field, tall trees forming a circle around the area. The sun illuminated them and the boulder they'd walked out of.

"Where to from here?" Declan asked. He looked toward Emma as if she were the leader. Yes, Alivia had given her the amulet but did that make her the leader?

"I think we need to go south toward the road, then west. Kylie..."

She was cut off as Bloodcloaks holding crossbows stepped out from behind the trees surrounding the grove. Several dark mages also revealed themselves. "Ambush!" Emma cried.

Emma and the others circled up, weapons drawn. Kylie and her mother summoned fire to their hands. Emma, without a weapon and unable to summon magic on command, felt useless in that moment.

"Ah, Samira," a female voice said. One of the hooded figures stepped into the light and pulled down her head.

Kylie's mother gasped. "Esmeralda?"

The red-haired woman smiled triumphantly at being recognized.

"Were you behind this?" Samira asked, pointing in the direction of the secret coven. "Did you betray the location of the coven?"

She shrugged. "What can I say? I was cast out and the dark mages took me in. Now, you're all going to come with us." She gestured and Bloodcloaks not armed with crossbows approached. Five of them withdrew silver collars from their belts. They looked identical to the collar Kylie had worn before. The girl backed up at the sight of them, turning their circle into an odd shape.

Emma thought about fighting but realized they were outnumbered. The crossbowmen would shoot them down with ease at a range of a few dozen feet and there were enough dark mages that they would overwhelm the meager, almost non-existent, abilities of Emma, Ethan and Richard and destroy Kylie and her mother. "Lower your weapons," she ordered the others.

"What?" Ethan asked. "You want to *let* them capture us?"

"Oh, precious boy," Esmerelda said before laughing. "You don't have a choice in the matter. Listen to your sister."

Sister? So she, and the dark mages, knew they were brother and sister? How did they find that out? Esmerelda hadn't been in the coven when they arrived. Was there a spy in the coven who had informed on them? She pushed the question aside and focused on the men approaching with dangerous instruments meant to stop them from using magic.

"Just do it," Emma growled.

She heard weapons clatter to the ground. The Bloodcloaks, emboldened by the helplessness of their prey, surged forward and roughly seized the members of the group in unison. One shoved Emma to the ground. Her face pressed into the dirt and she turned her head to spit dirt out. They could have gone easier on them, but what did she expect of murderers? And what was an order that supposedly hated "witches" doing working together with dark mages? Yet more questions she couldn't answer. A collar snapped around her neck and she felt "something" fading from her. Like a blanket being thrown over a lantern. Was that her magic? Or just her connection with it? Was it like putting a cup over a flame, temporary, or more like severing a rope? She assumed the former, since magic would return after removing a collar. The fact that she was thinking such analytical thoughts as she was taken captive bothered her. Why was she so calm in this moment? Before leaving Ironforge she would have been struggling to bite her captor and flee. Now she was taking it calmly. Had she changed so much? The soldier then bound her hands with rope as an extra precaution.

"You won't get away with this," Samira said boldly as she was tackled to the ground to Emma's left. It took two men to bring her down and she earned a kick in the ribs with her comment.

Esmerelda smiled. "Where you are going you won't be speaking so boldly. In fact, you might not ever speak intelligibly again. Bring them."

Chapter 15

The butt of a spear prodded Emma in the back. She resisted the urge to turn and glare at the Bloodcloak. The first time she'd done that it earned her a smack that sent her hurtling to the ground. Then the same guard had poked her until she got up and started walking again. Her face still stung.

Ahead loomed a stone fortress on a hill. The guards led their prisoners toward the iron-banded wood gates at the base of the hill while crossbowmen atop the walls and towers watched them approach.

"What fortress is this?" she whispered to Kylie, who walked in front of her.

Kylie shook her head slightly. "I don't know this area. We came southeast, and I grew up in the northwest."

"It's Senegal Fortress," Declan put in from behind Emma. "It was abandoned over five hundred years ago during the Fourth Galatian Wars. I'm glad those are over."

"Why was it abandoned?" Emma asked, not turning her head. It looked like a defensible position and the walls and gates were intact.

"It was deemed cursed after Count Elehar went mad and murdered his entire family atop the fortress and threw them to the ground below. He then set fire to the whole place."

"Oh," was all Emma was able to muster in response. Quite a gruesome history for the fortress.

"No one knows what drove the man mad. Let us pray we don't remain long enough to find out."

Emma shuddered. They had traveled for the better part of a day to reach this location. It was late afternoon now and the memory of Alivia and Charles sacrificing themselves played repeatedly in her mind.

Emma was sure they couldn't have survived the collapse of an entire cavern. What could she have done different? If only she'd been stronger. They shouldn't have even *gone* to the coven. Maybe then they could have been spared. But another part of her told her that was the wrong way of thinking about it. Alivia sacrificed herself to stop a deadly weapon from falling into enemy hands, though Emma didn't know what power it had, and that wouldn't have happened if they hadn't been there. On top of that, they'd been hunted by the Bloodcloaks and their dark mage allies. Charles would have surely died and they all might have been captured sooner had they not gone to the cavern. She tried to push aside her guilt and focus on what awaited them.

The traitorous witch, Esmerelda, rode a black horse at the head of a column of Bloodcloaks, dark mages and Emma and her companions. Was she a leader of some sort? Perhaps of the dark mages, while Rahman commanded the Bloodcloaks? It had been several years since she was cast out - she could have organized something behind the backs of the coven. She frequently glanced back and smiled wickedly, her eyes focused on Samira at the back of the line.

The gates creaked open and guards ushered the prisoners inside. The Bloodcloaks broke off and headed for what looked like barracks built into the bedrock of the hill supporting the fortress. Elsewhere, others of their kind sparred or lounged around drinking. Some of the soldiers straightened while others ignored the procession.

Up the hill the dark mages, prisoners and a smaller retinue of guards went. They arrived at a second gate atop the hill, this one directly before the fortress itself. Emma looked behind her out at the vast forest. She thought she could see the village they'd been attacked at to the northwest. She even thought she could see smoke to the far north, perhaps from Ironforge, but it may have been her imagination. The gate opened and they were shoved inside.

The fortress looming above them consisted of a circular central building towering against the mountainous backdrop flanked by four towers, one in each corner and connected by low walls. Each of the structures were constructed of black stone the likes Emma had never seen. Not that she was widely traveled, but she'd never seen stone that color in Ironforge. The stone also had no seams from where bricks were put together. Elaborate masonry her mother would have fawned over. Though if her mother were here it meant she too would be a captive, a thought which made Emma shiver.

The courtyard of the fortress housed no soldiers but dark cloaked figures. How many of the dark mages were there and where had they come from? How could such an organization have grown here unnoticed? They appeared to be entrenched, like they had been here for months or years.

Emma and the others were shoved up the stairs and prodded through a pair of dark double doors into the entryway of the fortress. The inside stood in stark contrast to the gruff exterior, with white marble floors polished to a sheen and a grand double staircase flanking a set of doors at the opposite end of the central building. Chandeliers hung from the ceiling while torches in gold sconces lined the wall. Doors peppered the sides, leading to unknown rooms. The group was moved, chains binding their hands clinking, toward the doors at the far end. Where were they being taken?

As they marched, Emma thought about her brother, up at the front of the line. She felt like she'd failed him. It had been *her* insisting they go to be trained at the Tower, and look where that got them. In shackles, consigned to an unknown fate. Did he feel betrayed by her? Or was he still mourning the loss of Jasmine only days earlier? She hadn't known her well and hadn't connected with her like he had. Had she been jealous of her "taking" her brother from her?

They entered through the dark double doors into a throne room of the same style as the entrance to the fortress only held up by wide marble columns. At the far end of the chamber a man sat on a throne as black as night. An unoccupied throne sat next to him. They were lined up in a row before him and a kick to each knee forced them to kneel. When Emma looked up her eyes were drawn to a blue orb on a pedestal in the corner. Black wisps swirled within it.

Esmerelda ascended the stairs and assumed the empty seat. She leaned to the side and the man, black-haired with a hook nose, kissed her on the cheek. He dismissed the Bloodcloaks with a wave, though the dark mages remained. His eyes swept over the group and Emma shivered when they focused on her for several seconds. "What have you brought us, Esmerelda?" he thundered.

"I come bearing gifts, my husband," she replied. "Sisters from the coven and 'mages' in training."

"Interesting," he replied, the word drawn out.

"Excuse me," Declan said, standing up and holding up a hand. "I am not a mage."

"Kneel, old man," the hook-nosed man ordered. "Or you will be of no use to me." He leaned forward. "Do you know what I do to those who are of no use to me?"

No use to him? Emma thought. Did that mean he had plans for them? She hadn't thought that far ahead as to their motivation. They could have killed them in the woods. That thought sent fear running through her.

Declan knelt. What had the fool man done that for? To stall for time? What good would that do when there was no one who even knew where they were?

"What of the mages from the Tower they traveled with?" he asked Esmerelda.

"They were killed in a cave-in of the coven."

The man raised an eyebrow at that. "A strange and foolish sacrifice. Not at all like her." He focused his gaze on Emma. "Why did she remain behind to be buried?"

Emma felt something tugging at her mind. The answer that Alivia had gone back to stop the Staff of Agamar from being taken welled up and threatened to come out. *No!* She thought furiously, fighting back the force. Was he trying to compel her to answer? Well, she refused! She gritted her teeth to keep from speaking and dared not even cry out as pain blossomed in her head. It felt as if she'd been hit by one of her mother's hammers. Her skull rung and she threatened to crumple to the floor, curl up in the fetal position and cry. Tears leaked from her eyes as the pain increased along with the urge to speak the truth to this man. She...had...to...resist!

"No!" she managed to get out in a half-shout, half-cry. "I...won't!"

The man smirked. "A strong-willed child. Few can resist my powers of persuasion." The pain and pressure in Emma's head disappeared and she felt like she could finally breathe normal again. His eyes moved on to Kylie and her mother and he flicked his gaze between them. "Ah, a mother and daughter?"

"Yes. She is one of the sisters," Esmerelda explained.

He reached out with a hand. Kylie's mother's hand went to her throat. She grabbed at it as if a noose were tightening. His cold gaze locked onto Kylie. "If you wish your mother to live, tell me what the mage was after. I can sense the secret beneath the surface of your thoughts. Let down your guard, child, or watch your mother die before your eyes."

"Mother!" Kylie shouted, hugging her mother. "Oh, please forgive me," she wept into her shoulder for several moments as her mother made gasping sounds. Then she raised her head and glared at the man. "She was after the Staff of Agamar. She wanted to keep it from the hands of the sisters or your order."

His eyes grew wide and his smile became sinister. "Excellent."

"Now you'll let my mother go?" Kylie asked.

"I shall release her." He squeezed his hand into a fist and Kylie's mother's eyes bulged as her throat closed completely. Bone snapped, and she collapsed into her daughter's arms.

"Mother!" Kylie screamed.

Emma gaped. Yes, she had seen death, but never close like this. She looked back at the dark-haired man. "You promised you would release her."

"And I did, child. I released her from this life. She goes to fight in the Great Beyond."

Kylie lowered her mother gently to the floor, then screamed in rage and stood. She began summoning magic - Emma could feel it even if she could not see it. She slapped her hands together and a cyclone of air swirled toward the man and Esmerelda.

He waved a hand and the wind evaporated. He snorted. "Is that the best you can do, child?" He made a tutting sound. "You have much to learn." He lifted a hand to dismiss the dark mages who had come forward. Emma sensed power radiating from them, suggesting they had been prepared to destroy Kylie at a word from their master. "But I admire your emotion, your heart. We will use that emotion to transform you." he sneered.

"I will never follow you," Kylie snapped.

Be quiet, Emma thought. She didn't want to lose anyone else today. "Kylie...," she warned.

"They all say that." He cast his arm out and gestured to the dark mages standing at attention in rows on both sides of the companions. "They all succumb." He sighed as the blue orb in the corner flashed. He cast out a hand and it floated to land in it. He focused and rubbed it three times and the orb transformed into the distorted head of a hooded figure. Emma could not see their face. "Report," the malevolent man sitting on the throne said. Emma still didn't know his name.

"My liege, I have been unable to determine the location of the gauntlet. I did learn the arch mage O'Leary set forth for Ironforge, though the reason is unclear. My allegiance is still secret."

"Good, good," the seated man said. His eyes flicked to Emma and back to the orb. "I have found the reason for arch mage O'Leary's trip. Continue your infiltration of the Tower and information gathering. We have found the Staff of Agamar but without the gauntlet it cannot be properly controlled."

"The staff has been found?" the man breathed. "Praise be to Rae'Shela." Declan drew a sharp intake of breath at the name and Emma wondered why.

"Indeed." He swiped his finger and the image disappeared, replacing by the inky clouds once more. He floated the orb back to its pedestal.

"Esmerelda, dear, order a contingent of mages to go to the ruins of the coven and find the staff." He snapped his fingers and pointed in the general direction of Emma. "Take them to the dungeons."

The dark mages this time taking the place of the Bloodcloaks, forced them to rise and turn their line back the way they'd come. Emma stopped in her tracks, forcing Kylie to run into her back. She turned boldly, disregarding her own mental advice to Kylie earlier. "What is your name?"

One of the dark mages immediately shoved her out of line and raised a hand to slap her. He paused at a raised hand by the seated man. "I shall answer her question. It is only right that my new acolytes know the name of their master." He leaned forward. "I am Zerrecia, loyal blood servant of Valdorf and follower of the mighty Rae'Shela."

Emma recognized neither of those names, other than the second from the servant shown in the looking orb. But she would not forget the name of their captor. She allowed herself to be shoved back into line and herded from the throne room.

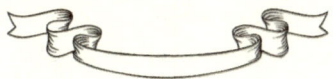

EMMA LOOKED AROUND her prison cell. Deep in the bowels of the fortress a row of cells held her and her companions. She and Kylie, who still sniffled after the loss of her mother, shared one cell, while the men shared the cell across the aisle. "Any bright ideas?" she asked, casting a wary glance toward the entrance to the prison where the mages guarding their block no doubt sat. All their possessions had been taken when they were first captured and they'd been lucky to retain the clothes on their back.

"Don't you have a hair pin or something?" Declan asked.

Emma rolled her eyes. "Does it look like I'm wearing my hair in any style?"

"Well, no," he paused and squinted toward Kylie in the dim fire light. "It *is* hard for my eyes to make anything out. What about the other girl?"

Emma considered the mess of hair draped down Kylie's face as she sobbed into her hands. "Not Kylie either."

"Ah, too bad."

"We have to use magic," Richard said.

"Brilliant observation," Declan said. "How many of you can melt iron? With a magic-nullifying collar on, I might add." No one spoke. "No one? Not even crying girl?"

"I just lost my mother," Kylie said through sobs. "Leave me alone."

Declan looked at the girl and pursed his lips. "Child, you will soon find that many people you love or care about shall die in your lifetime." His eyes drifted to meet Emma's. "Many." He smiled wide then. "But the good news is the pain passes."

"Not in two hours," Emma pointed out.

"It can if the alternative is *dying*," Declan pointed out. "We have a day, at most, before they find the Staff of Agamar and return. Once they return, bye-bye world as we know it."

Emma clenched her fists and came to clutch the bars of their cell. She directed her most irate expression toward Declan. "You have consistently known more than you let on, Declan. Spill the beans. What do you know that we do not? What do you know about the staff, this place, that Rae'Shela person, everything. Time to come clean."

She was taking a gamble. There was a chance he was just an innocent wagoner with delusions of grandeur. But her gut told her otherwise.

Declan sighed and rose stiffly. "You are observant, I will give you that, child." He sighed before continuing. "My name isn't Declan."

Not surprising, she thought. "Then what is it?"

"Favio." He gave a bow. "Court minstrel, traveling bard and the funniest man in the world." No one laughed at that statement. "All right, so perhaps that last bit is an exaggeration. But I *am* named Favio and my profession, officially, is as a bard."

"Why did you hide your identity?" The pieces clicked together in her mind. "Alivia knew who you were, didn't she?"

"Of course she did. I accompanied her on her journey. As to why I hid, well...there was some, let us say heat, a few years ago and I went into hiding to protect myself. I'm a survival-oriented person, you know."

"So all that stuff you said about being in palaces and the Tower, it was all true?"

"Every word. Well, mostly, I may have embellished."

"And what of the Staff of Agamar?"

"It is a cursed weapon."

"We got that from Alivia's reaction," Ethan said. He sat against the bars, back to Emma but looked up at Favio. "How is it cursed?"

"It dates to the Founding. A scientist," he frowned at their blank stares, "a man who creates new things, created a staff. But it was not just any staff. He imbued in it a gem. Inside that gem an artificial intelligence, like a being, lived. That artificial intelligence is the 'soul' of the weapon for lack of a better term. It allowed the weapon to tap into massive amounts of energy known as void energy which can be used to cast powerful spells beyond ordinary capability."

"That doesn't sound so bad," Emma said.

"There's more," Kylie groaned.

"Yes. Much more. All was well for centuries and the staff helped build wonders of the world such as the walls of Tar Ebon. But soon the staff became corrupted. Scholars aren't quite sure why, but people who wielded the staff, or were even near it, began to go mad. They lashed out in anger, made irrational decisions, a bit like drunks in that sense, and hurt those closest to them. The staff affected men with magic more than women and emitted a..." he paused, struggling for the correct word, "radiation they called it, a radiation that affected the minds of men. Women were less susceptible, but it nevertheless corrupted their bodies if they held it for too long. A great war was waged and the staff was supposedly lost. Or so the scholars thought. It appears it was hidden, instead." He looked to Kylie again. "Do you have anything more to add?"

"Our coven was given the sacred duty to protect the staff."

"Hence why you had no men with magic in your coven and why you kept it small on purpose - you didn't want to be discovered."

Kylie shook her head. "And now it is all for naught. Zerrecia will obtain the staff and become more powerful than we can imagine."

Emma made up her mind in that moment. She clutched the amulet hanging around her neck. "We have to do something."

"That is what I have been saying all along, child," Favio said. "Since neither of you have hair pins, let's keep thinking."

"What do we do if we escape?" Richard asked. "This place is crawling with soldiers and mages and none of us are trained."

"One bridge at a time, young man."

"You didn't answer my question about Rae'Shela," Emma said. "Who is he?"

"Ah," Favio's face fell. "An evil 'god' the enemies of mankind serve. Some poor unfortunate, well, gullible and evil, really, humans have also fallen into their cult. They're known as the Cult of Rae, for they worship the god Rae'Shela."

"But...we're all human," Emma said.

"He means the Krai'kesh," Ethan said.

"Oh." Memories of the stories their father used to read to them about the dark times before they were born and the Krai'kesh invasion came flooding back.

"Indeed. A great many lives were lost when the Krai'kesh came south. But their influence, it turns out, spread wider than we thought. Although the bulk of their forces were defeated, the worship of their god continued and spread like a plague. It culminated in their champion, Valdorf, taking the field against a band of heroes. They managed to defeat him by banishing him to the shadow realm and hid his gauntlet."

"That is the gauntlet Zerrecia mentioned," Emma surmised.

"Correct. Not only does it draw power stably from the shadow realm, it can interface with the staff, allowing the wielder to do so safely." He shrugged. "Look at me, talking science. It appears I spent too much time with Jason."

"Jason Thorpe?" Ethan asked. He always had cared about the stories of old more than she did.

"The very same," Favio smiled. "He yet lives, too, sailing the oceans last I heard. Smartest man I know, and I know a lot of men."

Emma pushed aside curiosity about the Krai'kesh and Eternals and focused on something else she'd seen in the throne room. "The orb, what was it?"

"A communication stone. The mages can use them to communicate across vast distances. There is only a fixed amount of them in existence. The Tower has one, but I am sure that henchman wasn't using the Tower's stone. The Cult must have obtained a stone through different means."

"Could we use the stone? To call for help from the Tower?"

Favio stroked his chin. "In theory, I suppose." He snapped his fingers. "Yes, that could work. Send out a call for help, the mages...hmmm...they wouldn't get here in time to save us."

"But at least they would have warning," Emma said. "We can send the warning and find a way to escape. Keep running until we get to safety." *And if we can't escape, we sacrifice ourselves. It's what Mom and Dad would do.*

"That is true," Favio agreed. "So how do we escape?"

"I don't know."

"You do not want to escape," a female voice said from a room with a door at the end of the row of cells. The doored room stood in contrast with the barred layout of the cells holding Emma and her companions. She had assumed the room was unoccupied, which in hindsight was foolish.

"Who are you?" Emma asked.

"My name does not matter. What you should know is escape is not something to desire in this place."

"Why not?"

"Because they toy with you. They *allow* you to escape only to catch you, tear you asunder and throw you back in here."

"Sounds like someone's had experience," Favio said. He waved a hand toward the cell. "Is there anyone else in there with you?" Was he worried about someone overhearing him revealing his true name?

"They are all gone. Taken by the darkness. To serve *him*. I am the last."

"How long have you been down here?" Emma asked. No windows graced the walls of the cells, making it difficult to judge time, but torches hung on the walls and surely they would need to be changed at intervals and prisoners fed, right? That could allow a prisoner to get a sense of time.

"Years," she said. "Or more, I do not know." She cackled. "I am the last, the last, the last."

"I think she may be insane," Favio said. "Perhaps that's why they didn't want her," he said under his breath in a quieter tone loud enough for Emma to hear but not the unnamed woman.

"Why did they spare you?" She remembered the feeling of pressure in her mind. "Or how did you resist?"

"Spared?" she asked incredulously. "I was not spared, child. Living in this place is worse than death. You shall see, you shall see."

"We're getting out of here," Emma said, feeling less confident than she sounded. "Can you help us?"

"Should a woman help fools who wish to die? No, I cannot help you."

"Let us worry about our foolishness and possible fate. Please, help us," Emma retorted. They just had to get out and they'd have a fighting chance. If this woman and her people had escaped, multiple times, there had to be a way. "We will take you with us. Even if that means you want to die."

"You would kill me?"

Emma was aghast. "No, of course we wouldn't kill you. I just meant..."

"Only death is an escape for me. If you cannot give me death I cannot help you."

"*I* will take your life," Favio began, "if you help us escape."

Emma gaped at Favio. What was he saying? He would murder someone in cold blood?

"You have a deal," the woman said. "Girl, there is a stone in the wall behind you that is loose. Find it."

Emma strained to see the woman's face in the gloom of the dungeon but could not. Clearly she was watching them, right? She nodded, went to the wall and ran her hand across the rough stone. Here the stone was not seamless like it had been on the outside. What did that mean? Was part of the fortress older than others? She tried pushing on stones, but none budged. At last, after going from top to bottom and side to side for what seemed like an hour Emma found a stone with no mortar around it. "I found it," she reported.

"Excellent," the woman's voice came. "Remove the stone and twist the lever within."

Emma squeezed her fingers into the space around the loose stone and, getting a firm grip, pulled. It wouldn't move. "Will you help me, Kylie?" she asked.

Kylie sat where she was, head hung down. Did she fall asleep or had she heard any of the discussions so far at all?

"Fine, I'll do it myself," she said. She tugged again. The stone budged a little. After a few tries the stone slid out. She reached her hand into the gap and felt a metal rod. She gripped it and turned the lever. She felt a vibration behind the stone and a series of clinks echoing from the hole. The vibration continued down through the wall into the floor and cascaded until it reached the door. With a click the door mechanism engaged. Emma crept toward it warily and looked around.

Favio nodded encouragement while Ethan and Richard watched with anticipation.

She pushed at the door. It slid open without resistance. "That is a neat trick," she said. "Who builds a secret lever into a prison cell?"

Favio snapped his fingers. "The king who once ruled here. He was a famous drunk and when in his cups he would commit horrendous crimes. Legend says he ordered his guards to lock him in the dungeon at night to sleep after he'd had too much drink so that he would not go out and murder innocent farm girls in the surrounding countryside. Then in the morning he could simply pull the lever and walk out to resume his duties as king."

"That sounds like a pretty crappy king," Ethan commented.

"Indeed, but for centuries kings were chosen by 'divine right.' How they determined which divine beings granted these rights is beyond me."

"How do I get the others out?" she asked the woman.

"Yes, do we have a lever of our own?" Favio asked hopefully.

The woman laughed. "You must get the key from the guards."

Emma groaned. Easier said than done. She looked back at Kylie. Had she even noticed they were free? "Kylie, come on."

"I'm sure you can do it yourself," Kylie said, a bitter note in her tone.

Emma clenched her fists and rounded on the girl. "Listen. I was the first to defend you when Favio said you should get over your emotions. But I realize now he's *right*. Now is not the time to be mourning your mother. So suck it up and push the emotions you're feeling aside. You can mourn when we're out of this place. Deal?"

Kylie looked up, anger mingling with pain. She opened her mouth to speak but then looked at the open door and snapped it shut. She focused on Emma's face and the anger *and* pain evaporated. "You're right." She cleared her throat. "How can I help?"

Emma held up a finger. "One moment." She turned toward the door keeping the woman locked away. "Do you know when the guards change watch or anything else about their behavior?" She walked slowly toward the door, hoping to catch a glimpse of her.

"I only know they empty the chamber pot once a day and feed me twice a day," she said.

Emma reached the door and came face-to-face with an older woman with graying hair frayed and twisting in every direction.

"Hello, child," the woman said. Scars marred her face and the scraps of clothing she wore looked like they hadn't ever been washed. "Did you want to see if I was real?"

"I wanted to make sure this wasn't a trap."

"Even if it were a trap, did you have much choice in the matter? You were already captive, what would be worse?" The woman was right, of course. They had to take risks if they wanted to reap the reward. In this case the reward was their potential freedom instead of whatever the Cult of Rae had planned for them.

"We need to get these collars off. How did Alivia remove yours, Kylie?"

"She used magic to remove it. It's one of the only ways I know to remove it. That or a pry-bar strong enough to break the link physically. The collars are made of a soft metal."

"And since neither of us have magic with collars on..." They were stuck without magic and no way to remove the collars.

Kylie crept toward the door leading out of the prison block. She peaked through the hole and quickly dropped her head down. She waited until Emma crept next to her to speak. "Two guards, playing cards at a table. They each have a sword."

Swords. Emma snapped her fingers. "We could use their swords to break the seals on our collars."

"But how would we get the swords from the guards?"

Emma eyed their cell. "I have an idea."

"HELP!" EMMA CRIED AT the top of her lungs. "Help, she's dying!"

They were back in their cells and Kylie pretended to moan and writhe in pain on the floor.

Moments later the door leading to the block opened and a guard stepped inside, sword drawn. "What's all the racket?" he demanded.

"She's dying!" Emma shouted again, pointing to Kylie. "Please, help."

The guard, an ordinary Bloodcloak and not a dark mage, waved a hand to dismiss her concern. "She'll survive until morning." He turned to leave.

"She won't live that long," Emma said. "Zerrecia took a special interest in her. If she dies on your watch he won't be happy."

That got the guards attention. He groaned and came over to the cell. He removed a key and unlocked it, then stepped inside. He didn't kneel right away, instead he looked at Kylie, studying her. "What's wrong with her?"

Kylie groaned and screamed in pain in response to his question. She grabbed at her stomach and then her head and then her chest, suggesting widespread pain or multiple medical symptoms. None of that mattered to the guard though, for he was already convinced he had a dying woman on his hands and his eyes had widened in panic. He knelt.

Emma fingered the brick in her hand. Taking one final glance at the door the guard entered through, and feeling fortunate the old woman was right and the other guard wouldn't join him, she hefted the heavy object and swung. Whack.

The Bloodcloak fell forward, blood pooling at the back of his head. He fell on top of Kylie.

"Oof," Kylie said. "You just had to make him land on me, didn't you?"

"Sorry," Emma said, suppressing a smile. She helped roll the big man off her friend. They were still friends, weren't they? Sure they'd exchanged words, but wasn't that the mark of friendship? She set that thought aside and grabbed the sword hilt. She withdrew the blade and held it up. "So do I just, what, stick this under the collar and pull?"

"If you want to decapitate me, sure," Kylie said. "Give it to me, I'll show you."

Emma handed the weapon over. "Please hurry," she reminded her.

Kylie lined the place against Emma's collar. "There's a seam, right here." She pressed the tip of the blade forward and Emma felt pressure as the collar pressed into her skin. "I have to press slowly so I don't stab you when the collar..." the collar snapped open and fell to the ground. Emma felt a sharp pain in her neck coupled with a chill running down her spine that she guessed was her magic returning to her.

"Ow," she complained. "Did you just stab me?" She raised a hand to her neck and felt something sticky and wet there. She looked at it and found a streak of red staining it. "You stabbed me!"

"It's just a nick," Kylie replied.

"Yes, I've had worse shaving," Favio said. "Now would you kindly remove Kylie's and perhaps come free us?"

Emma unlocked the door to their cell and ran across to unlock the other cell. She tossed the keys to Favio. "Let the old lady out." She pointed at his face. "Don't you dare kill her."

Favio offered a flamboyant bow. "I will not kill her at this time."

"Good enough," Emma replied sarcastically. She returned to Kylie and took the sword from her. "Stand still." She found the seam after several moments and lined the tip of the blade on it. She pressed on it, trying to maintain even pressure to not stab her in return. The collar didn't separate. She pressed harder until at last the collar separated. She tried to stop the blade from passing through the space the seam had occupied and stabbing Kylie but found it was not as easy as she'd imagined. The blade *did* poke Kylie, though Emma told herself it wasn't as deep as her own cut.

A sigh of relief emerged from Kylie. "Thank you." She smiled at Emma.

"Yeah, don't mention it. Watch the door. That second guard might show up any second and you're the only one of us who can control their magic on command."

Kylie nodded and squared herself toward the door, remaining vigilant.

Emma crossed back to the boys' cell where Ethan and Richard waited nonchalantly while Favio free the old woman. She cautiously freed the two boys from their collars.

"Thanks, sis," Ethan said. "Didn't even nick me."

"Practice," Emma replied. She performed the same bloodless maneuver on Richard a moment later. Then she handed the sword hilt-first to Richard. "Here, you know how to use this the best."

Richard took the blade and nodded. "Mind if I take the scabbard from the guard?"

Emma shrugged. "Go for it." She hesitated. "Just don't kill the guy."

"I think he may already be dead," Richard said, crossing over and looking at the head wound. "He's breathing, but he might not live that much longer."

Emma felt a twinge of guilt at that news. Yes, he was an enemy, but not every person fighting for an evil cause deserved to die. Sometimes they were semi-honest people trying to make a living or were brainwashed into serving an evil cause. Still, there was no time for regret, they had to find that communication stone and fast.

Favio led the old woman out of her cell. "Judith here is ready to go."

Emma nodded at the woman. "It's a pleasure to meet you, Judith."

"I still think you're fools," she replied, though a small smile softened the words. "But I'll follow along and see your stupidity first-hand."

"Prepare to be pleasantly surprised," Emma said. "Richard, will you remove her collar?" Once he finished, surprisingly with no blood on Judith's neck, she surveyed her companions and took a deep breath. "All right, here's the plan..."

Chapter 16

The lone remaining guard had still not entered by the time Emma finished detailing the plan which formed in her mind. Kylie swept out of the room, eyes white and magic swirling within her. Emma could still not *see* how she was using her magic very well, but she could sense her use of magic and saw the results. The result in this case being the guard catching a fire ball to the chest. His screams died in his chest as his lungs burned in an instant. Kylie's face showed no remorse as she walked past the charred guard.

"Lead us to the passage," she instructed Judith.

The old woman led them down a passage and around a bend. Emma kept her ears perked for any sound of clinking metal or voices which would indicate guards. At last they arrived at a suit of armor flanked by two torches. The woman twisted the gauntlet of the armored husk and the pedestal holding the ancient suit depressed into the wall and slid aside, revealing a dark passageway.

Emma snatched a torch from the wall while Ethan took the other. He and Richard formed their rearguard. If they ran into trouble Emma wanted Richard's hands free to fight with the blade. She took a deep breath. "Let's go. We have less than an hour before the changing of the guards gives us away." They plunged into the dark passageway.

With Judith's help they navigated the warren of passageways. Emma got the sense of going up at a gentle incline. At certain intervals the rough stone would give way to smooth slabs of stone before transitioning back to rough stone. Were those other entrances?

"What were these?" she asked.

"Servant passages," Favio said from ahead of Ethan and Richard. "Nobles don't like to see filthy servants traversing the halls. So they relegate them to the shadows or, in this case, the walls."

"How did you know this was here, Judith?"

"I told you, child, we escaped many times. I learned the secret entrances during such desperate flights. Flights that ultimately failed."

"Well, this one won't fail." Emma ignored the memory of Favio promising to kill Judith if they failed to escape.

Judith harrumphed in response. She brought them to a crossroad in the tunnel and then to the right. "This path leads to the throne room. But there will likely be guards."

"Not if Zerrecia isn't there," Emma reasoned. "He has to sleep some time, right? And it's night time."

"For now. Dawn is less than an hour away. What's the backup plan?" Favio asked.

"There is no backup plan." *Thanks for the vote of confidence, Favio,* she thought.

After several minutes they arrived at a section of smooth stone. An empty sconce sat to the right of the door. Judith pulled it down and twisted. Emma closed her eyes and held her breath, expecting shouts of alarm and cries of battle. None came. Emma opened her eyes and peeked out. The throne room was empty and, fortunately, the communication orb was there on its pedestal like before. "All clear," she said to the others. She placed her torch in the empty sconce Judith had pulled and exited the hidden passage. The others followed her out. Through the vast windows behind the throne she saw the mountains illuminated in the pre-dawn light.

"You four watch the door," she pointed to Kylie, Richard, Ethan and Favio. "You're the best shot we have once word gets out we've escaped. We already burned much of an hour traversing the secret passages."

Favio saluted. "Of course, m'lady."

"Judith, come with me." Emma walked toward the communication stone. "I may need help using the stone and I'm hoping you'll know something about it."

"I have never used such a device," Judith admitted. "But I will offer what assistance I can." She followed Emma at a slow pace.

Emma studied the stone. The black splotches within continued to swirl, unaware of or unperturbed by her presence. Which of course made sense, since it wasn't like the stone had an awareness, right? "Should I touch it?" she asked.

Judith put her face close to the stone, studying the black spots within. "You say the dark one used this to communicate with someone in Tar Ebon?"

"Yes. It flashed and he activated it."

"Do you remember how he did so?"

"No, but..." she reached out with both hands. "Here it goes."

"Wait!" Judith said, slapping her hand. "Gather your magic before touching it. I suspect it requires magic, since it is an ancient communication device of magic-users only."

"Oh, right." That made sense. Emma closed her eyes and concentrated, willing the magic to rise within her. A chill that gave way to warmth began in her head and spread down her body. It tingled through her arms and felt like it pooled in her fingers. It filled her chest and meandered down her legs and made her toes tingle. She could see the elements of existence laid out before her. The elements of stone in the wall, the elements of copper and zinc in the brass pedestal. On and on her perception spread. She felt more alive than she ever had before. *I'm ready.* She placed her hands on the orb and felt a jolt of energy surge through her and the orb turned pitch black.

The torchlight, orb, windows, mountains, floor and ceiling seemed to fall away around her. She almost let go of the orb in her shock, but something told her not to let go. She stood in a void, her body visible to her but more translucent than reality. She felt formless, like she could blow away at the slightest push from a soft summer breeze. *What is this place?* She wondered.

"Which stone would you like to communicate with and what is your message?" a voice asked. It did not sound human. Instead it sounded as if the most dull, bored person in the world were speaking.

"Ummm...the stone at the Tower of the Seven Stars. And my message is..."

"Error. You must specify which stone at the Tower you wish to communicate with. There are many devices near Tar Ebon."

"How do I differentiate?" she asked.

"You must speak the name of the stone," the voice asked. "Each stone has a unique identifier."

"Can you give me an example?"

"One moment." The voice paused before speaking several moments later. "Here is an example: 'The Cerulean Stone, the Crimson Stone, the Vermilion Stone.'"

"Are those stones at Tar Ebon?"

"I can provide a list of stones located near the city called Tar Ebon if you wish."

"Yes please."

"Here is a list: The Garish Stone, the Aquamarine Stone, the Stone of a Thousand Faces, the Shadow Stone, the Evergreen Stone and the Blood Stone."

"A lot to choose from. Which are the most active?"

"I cannot discern that," the voice said.

"Please, I must reach someone at the Tower."

"Please make a selection and I will attempt to connect you."

Emma frowned. Was the voice she spoke to human or some sort of construct? Its voice displayed no emotion and never changed. "Are you a human?"

"No. I am an artificial intelligence."

"What is that?" She remembered Favio telling them about the artificial intelligence in the gem on the Staff of Agamar. Was this similar?

"I am a machine capable of performing complex functions at a user's request. My primary function is to connect with other communication stones."

Emma's head spun. An artificial intelligence? Like some sort of alien of old inside an orb. She had an idea. "Can you communicate with more than one stone at once?"

"Emma!" a voice, a human voice, Ethan's voice, interrupted her conversation. She looked around but saw no one else. "Emma!" the voice shouted again.

"What?" Emma responded.

"They're coming. Please hurry. We'll hold them off as long as we can."

"I do not recognize the command 'what.' Would you like me to repeat my previous answer to your inquiry?"

"Yes, please." She hadn't heard the artificial intelligence's answer.

"Communication with multiple stones is possible but partners you initiate communication with cannot connect to other partners you are also connected with."

"Okay..." Emma said. She didn't understand what the AI had said.

"Would you like me to connect to all available stones at Tar Ebon?"

"Hurry, Emma!" Ethan's voice again interrupted. Why couldn't she hear the others?

"Yes, connect to all."

"Connecting. One moment please. Thank you for your patience."

The void pulsed and 6 balls of light appeared spaced out in a line before her. They pulsed in unison a moment after the void pulsed, as if responding to it. This pulsing rhythm continued for several moments. What was the AI waiting for?

"When will I know to speak?" she asked.

"When a connection is established a stone will cease pulsing and solidify," the voice clarified.

The pulsing continued. None had gone solid yet. "Why aren't any changing to solid?" she asked.

"No one has answered yet."

"Can they tell who is calling? Can they see me?"

"They do not have that capability. They may be distracted or otherwise indisposed." It was morning, after all, there was a chance all the mages were asleep. Fear caused the breath to catch in her throat. What if the saboteur traitor mage was the only one to answer? Despair fell upon her and she was about to give up when one ball of light turned from flashing blood red to solid. She'd connected!

The solid red orb morphed into a human figure. An older Sagami man with a top-knot and wearing traditional robes Emma had seen in picture books her father had at the shop stood there. He squinted. "Who are you?"

"My name is Emma," she began. "Please, I need help."

"How did you connect to my stone?"

"I am using a communication stone and asked to connect to the stones located in Tar Ebon."

"Young lady, there is protocol to this. I do not know you and this is unauthorized communication. Is this a prank?"

"What? No, no," Emma held up her hands to support her innocence. "We were traveling with Alivia O'Leary when we were attacked and..."

He held up a hand. "Alivia you say? Where is she? Let me speak with her."

Emma looked down, though her feet had disappeared in the voice. "She died."

"A convenient excuse."

"It's not an excuse!" Emma blurted without thinking. "She died protecting the Staff of Agamar."

The man's eyes went wide. "The Staff of..." his eyes narrowed. "This must be a trick. The Staff of Agamar has been lost to history for centuries."

"It was found in a coven of witches. They protected it."

"A likely story, but I will not let you trick me into revealing..."

"She gave me this," Emma hurried to say, sensing that the man would shut down his side of the communication if she didn't convince him of the truth. She withdrew the amulet with the locket Alivia had given her moments before going to her death. "She gave me this." She held it out for the man.

He stepped forward, eying it with suspicion and lifting spectacles to inspect it. He opened it and read something within. He snapped it shut and flipped the locket over. "It does *seem* authentic. You say Alivia gave it to you?"

Emma nodded. "Yes."

The man sighed, handed the amulet back and crossed his arms. He did not return to where he had previously been standing. "All right. Let's say I believe you. What danger are you in?"

"We have been captured by the Cult of Rae. Their leader, Zerrecia, has sent men to retrieve the Staff of Agamar from the ruins of the coven that protected it. We are trapped in a fortress near the eastern mountains, southeast of Ironforge," she said as she remembered the distant smoke she had seen.

The man's eyes went wide. "The Cult of Rae. We must do something!" he exclaimed.

At that moment, one of the other lights which had been flashing, a black orb as dark as midnight, solidified. It morphed into a man with a hood veiling his face. He saw Emma and shouted "You!"

Emma backed away, her hand leaving the orb on the pedestal.

"What is it?" the Sagami master said.

Couldn't he see this new, dark-clothed man? She remembered the warning the AI had given her. People she connected with could not see one another. "Someone new," she answered.

"And you are an intruder," the hooded man said. "You've stolen the stone! Leave this place now!" A pressure surrounded her, threatening to send her flying into the void. She held on but only barely.

"I don't have much time," she hurried, ignoring the hooded man. "Please send help!" Even as she spoke the image of the older man was fading. He spoke but no words came out. Was the hooded man blocking her communication?

"Leave!" the man screamed, and Emma felt herself flying backward, the orbs becoming distant specks of light that blinked out of existence. She could no longer see even the orb she had touched to come to this place. She tumbled, unable to right herself with no landmark to focus on. She screamed into the void, willing herself to leave that place. Nothing happened.

Her spin halted abruptly as a hand grabbed hers. A woman, clothed in black and with shadow veiling her face floated there. "You came too far. You should not be here."

"I just...I just wanted to communicate," Emma stammered. "We need help."

"Yes, yes, I heard your conversation," the woman said impatiently. "Help will be coming soon. Can you survive that long?" Even as she spoke the space around them seemed to move and they were back at the blue orb with black specks on the brass pedestal. "Touch the orb and you'll return to the physical realm."

"Thank you," Emma said, but when she turned around the woman was gone. She rushed to touch the orb and felt relief as the void transformed into the throne room. She found Judith staring at her.

"Ah, child, you have returned. I feared for your soul."

"Did I go too far?" Emma asked.

The woman shrugged. "The stones can be dangerous. They transfer your voice but can take your soul."

"Why didn't you warn me?"

"Would you have touched it if I had?"

Emma wanted to say yes, that she would have touched it regardless of the risk. But would she really? Would she have gone so far into the void, or the shadow realm, as that woman had called it, if she knew her soul was on the line? She was spared an answer by a crash coming from the door to the throne room.

The wooden doors bulged inward, as if struck by a battering ram. Kylie stood several meters from it, arms stretched out and hands flayed wide. Emma felt power emanating from her. Was she reinforcing the door? Her own mind felt too tired to tap into her magic and see what the girl was doing. Ethan and Richard stood behind her, both with swords. Ethan having received his from the burned guard. Favio leaned against a pillar, an unconcerned expression on his face as he noticed Emma. "Ah, the valiant hero returns. Did you send the message?"

Emma nodded. "Yes, I met a mage from the Tower. But we were cut off by one of Zerrecia's spies. I was saved by..." Another boom from the door cut her off. It wasn't important - she survived and was standing there, that's what counted. "What's going on?"

Favio jerked his head back to indicate the door. "A whole bunch of enemies on the other side of those doors. Kylie's holding the door together but it's only a matter of time before it splinters and we're toast."

"We need to find a way out," Emma mumbled. She looked to the secret passage. "How about the way we came?"

"We were just waiting on you, ma'am."

"Stop calling me ma'am," Emma said, half-serious and half-joking. "Kylie, Richard, Ethan, it's time to go!"

Ethan and Richard whipped their heads toward her, then Ethan tapped Kylie on the shoulder and spoke to her. Kylie started backing away from the door, arms still raised. Ethan guided her so she wouldn't bump into a stone column and in less than a minute they all met at the door to the secret entrance.

"When I let go the door will shatter. We will have a moment to escape and shut the door," Kylie said with effort.

"Everyone inside," Emma ordered. The old woman didn't move. Instead she began walking toward the bulging door. "Where are you going, Judith?"

"I will hold the door for a little longer," she said. "Release it to me, child." She put a hand on Kylie's shoulder.

"No. You're coming with us," Emma said.

"If they enter and no one is here they will be suspicious and find the secret passage sooner. If they find me they will be distracted long enough to give you distance." She gave a wan smile. "Besides, this is fulfilling my wish. You're off the hook, bard."

Favio stepped out from the secret passage and gave a bow. "It was an honor knowing you, even if it was such a fleeting time, Judith."

The old woman walked to where Kylie had been standing before and held up her hands. Some sort of hand-off must have taken place, for Kylie slumped and took a deep breath. "She's taken it over. We can go."

Emma made sure she was the last through the door, then she twisted the sconce and pushed it against the wall. The door slid shut and she removed the torch. Ethan already held his again. He gestured. "Your lead."

The group had gone perhaps twenty feet when a boom shook the wall. Dust fell from the ceiling. The door had been broken. Distant screams echoed through the walls and then silence. Judith was gone.

Down they went, trying to find a balance between stealth and speed. Kylie tripped once but Favio helped her to her feet. Ethan looked back several times as they went, likely paranoid they would be caught.

Soon they reached an unfamiliar section of the secret passage. *Down, keep going down*, Emma thought. Nowhere would be safe to emerge unless they were down as far as they could go. They didn't know the layout of the fortress but if these passages were built for servants it made sense they would stretch all the way to the barracks currently housing the Bloodcloaks on the ground level.

Her theory was proven correct when the passage ended in a dead-end. A single slab of stone stood along the wall to their right, flanked again by wall sconces. Emma braced herself to twist the sconce, but this time she expected shouts of alarm when the door slid open. She twisted and pulled and the door slid open. Darkness met their eyes on the other side of the hidden entrance. She crept forward and looked out. Fabric met her eyes. A wall hanging? Voices came to her ears - gruff voices - soldier voices.

"Soldiers," she whispered to the others. "We're behind a wall hanging."

"Then we have the element of surprise," Richard said unexpectedly. He didn't speak often, preferring to loom like a gentle giant. She didn't think he disliked them, but was perhaps shy. He withdrew the sword from his scabbard taken from the first guard.

She hated saying this but, "we're not killing them if we can help it."

"They wouldn't hesitate to kill us," Ethan countered.

"I know that," Emma explained patiently. "But if we start killing them we waste time and give them an opportunity to call for reinforcements." She pointed to Kylie. "She can do a lot, but she can't hold off dozens of dark mages and those," she pointed at the sword Ethan held also, "will be virtually useless against magic."

"Not if we get the drop on them."

"I hate to interrupt this wonderful sibling spat, but we're racing daylight," Favio said.

He was right. Once the sun rose any chance they had of escaping unnoticed would evaporate like fog in sunlight. "Let me look." She went to the edge of the wall curtain and peeked around it. They had entered in a secluded, semi-enclosed chamber. A wall ran to her right and ran along until it ended abruptly. The room had 3 sides but the fourth was open. A desk sat in front of the wall curtain. Perhaps officer quarters? Odd quarters with limited privacy, but they were fortunate it was unoccupied. For how long was another question. She returned and briefed the others on what she'd seen.

"Let's go into the office and go from there," Favio suggested. "Every step that takes us away from the guards shouting through the secret passages is good with me." He stepped out and the others followed. Emma triggered the sconce on their side of the door and it slid shut. Hopefully, with the guards not knowing which door they exited through, they would retain the element of surprise.

The group lined up against the wall and again Emma was the one to look around the corner. She wondered why it was always *her* being the scout and not one of the others. Favio would make a good scout. The next corner would be his to look around. Around this corner she found a hallway with dim sunlight streaming in through a door at the end. The voices came from a room further down the hall on the left. A mess hall? Or the armory? She didn't know, but the voices were concentrated there. "We have one chance," she said. "We have to make it to the end of this hall without getting noticed. Be ready for anything," she looked at Kylie, Richard and Ethan.

"I'll lead," Richard volunteered.

Emma opened her mouth to protest but the hulking man was already rushing down the hall. Emma and the others followed. Richard slowed as he approached the room the voices came from. He looked around the corner, gave a thumbs up to the group and strolled past the doorway.

When Emma approached the doorway she too peeked inside the vast mess hall with soldiers eating, drinking and joking with one another. She heaved a sigh of relief. Then one of the soldiers glanced toward the doorway. His eyes went wide. "Hey!" he mouthed, the room being too loud for her to hear his exact words. He pointed in her direction, alerting the others at his table. Emma, froze in surprise, remained where she was until the entire table full of Bloodcloaks were looking at her.

"Shit," she said. "Run!" she commanded her compatriots, breaking into a run. Footsteps told her the others got the message. They caught up with Richard and she shoved him forward. "Run, they've seen us!"

The group raced to the end of the tunnel and, without stopping to look, burst into the pre-dawn light. This close to the mountains, dawn was slow in coming, with the sun only then passing to the south and spreading its light toward the fortress walls. Said light illuminated a group of Bloodcloaks returning from patrol, with the gates wide open. This was their chance!

"To the gate!" Emma shouted. Behind them, shouting came from the direction of the mess hall. She didn't dare glance back.

The Bloodcloak patrol spotted them, too, and drew their weapons. Shouts rose from the wall, though they were directed outward, with guards atop the stone battlement pointing outward.

Emma skidded to a halt, Richard to the right, Ethan to the left. Kylie and Favio brought up the rear.

"I don't mean to put a damper on this escape attempt," Favio began. "But we are being pursued. Why are we stopping?"

"Kylie needs to stand still to cast magic, don't you?"

Kylie nodded. "Yes, I do."

"Can you take care of the patrol so we can get through the gates?"

"What then?" Ethan asked. "The guards will just shoot at us." He pointed toward the crossbows held by the men who were paying them no mind.

"Something is distracting them," Emma said, pointing. "We have to take the chance. Kylie?"

Kylie's eyes went white and Emma felt her drawing upon her magic. The mounted guards kicked their horses into a run, preparing to run the group down. Emma felt the urge to close her eyes against the coming onslaught but at the last moment a wall of wind slammed into them. Men and horse tangled together as they flew and fell several meters to the right.

"Now!" Emma shouted, running for the gates. The gates began to close. *No, no, no,* and new voices came from behind them. A glance back revealed dark mages running down the hill. She felt magic building and braced herself for a counterstrike from their enemy. But instead of fire or ice or another type of attack striking the group the fire flashed *over* the walls. What was out there?

Chapter 17

Alivia stood at the edge of the woods facing the fortress. A glowing orb of light hovered above her head. Arrows and bolts flew toward her and slammed into an invisible wall to join the graveyard of wood and metal at her feet. The fireball Emma saw peeled apart as it flew until it extinguished before reaching her.

Emma felt a surge of hope at seeing their teacher. They'd thought her lost. No one should have been able to survive the cave in, right? She made for the woman and as she neared the orb of light resolved into an orb of light attached to a staff held aloft by Alivia. The Staff of Agamar.

"Is that..." Ethan began.

"Alivia!" Favio shouted.

Another salvo of bolts and arrows flew over their heads, supported this time by a ball of ice. Emma flinched. How soon before the men on the walls targeted *them* instead of the woman holding a bright glowing staff? She put her thought aside as they reached the forest's edge and passed beyond Alivia.

"Alivia," Emma said, huffing and puffing. Her side ached. She wasn't out of shape by any means, but sprinting for hundreds of meters while being chased by enemy soldiers would tire anyone out. "How..." was all she got out before launching into a coughing fit.

"The staff protected me," Alivia said, not looking at them. She remained facing the fortress, eyes white. Her voice sounded...off. Distant.

Emma stepped up to her and was about to embrace her when she spotted something black on the woman's arm. She looked up. Black ribbons ran down the arm holding her staff, looking like tattoos. They disappeared beneath her tunic but re-appeared around the base of her neck and at the elbow of her other arm. "What happened to you?" She pointed to the black lines. "Are you hurt?"

She finally turned her head and white eyes appraised Emma. "I am feeling fine. In fact, I feel more powerful than I ever have."

Emma swallowed. She met Ethan's eyes, which were as wide as hers. Favio met her gaze with a worried one of his own. "Have you ever seen anything like this?" she asked Kylie.

Kylie frowned. "Only in legend. It is said the staff drives men mad and corrupts female wielders."

"Corrupts them how?"

"A blood sickness." She pointed to the black lines. "Those are her veins, corrupted by the magic of the staff."

"So...much...power!" Alivia shouted, pumping her arm to shake the staff. Lightning shot forth in countless streaks to strike the guards on the walls. A fireball launched toward her by the dark mages changed direction in flight and hurtled back from whence it came. The enemy mages blocked the blow with their own shields but would have been shaken by the reality of their own magic being redirected against them.

The outer walls shook. What did she have in mind? "Alivia, we need to go," Emma reminded her. "Thank you for rescuing us, but we can't stay here."

"I will destroy them all." Alivia acted as if she hadn't heard Emma's words.

Emma again reached her hand out, intending to shake her teacher, but hesitated because of the darkness. Still, *something* had to be done.

Motion from the gate of the fortress caught her attention. The guards from the barracks rushed out of the gates, likely driven by officers or dark mages. They looked nervous but held their swords at the ready. They charged forward. To their deaths, as it turned out, for Alivia leveled her staff at them and the ground opened to swallow them, and their screams, whole before closing.

"Nothing can stop her," Emma observed.

"Do we want to?" Richard asked. "I mean, if she destroys the whole fortress there's no one left to chase us, right?"

The man had a point. What did they care if enemies of the realm were slain by a mage of Tar Ebon? They would be doing the Federation a service. But no, many of the dark mages were ex-prisoners who had been converted and who knew what the situation of the Bloodcloaks really was.

"What if they overwhelm her?" she asked.

As if 'they' had been summoned, a group of dark mages led by a tall man in black armor, Zerrecia, emerged. He held what appeared to be a scepter in his hands.

Alivia raised her staff and lightning again streamed from it. The result was different this time, however, for the lightning hit its own barrier and flowed into the ground. The dark mages had organized a defense.

"You may have the staff," Zerrecia's voice boomed. "But we have the numbers. This ground will be your grave." He pointed his scepter toward them and a blast of wind infused with lightning swirled toward the group. The other dark mages sent fire and ice streaming toward them on the flanks.

Emma felt her eyes growing wide. *This is it. This is the end*, she thought.

Alivia leveled her staff again and a barrier blocked the lightning wind and the fire and ice. But instead of stopping, the attackers redoubled their efforts. More and more magical attacks struck the barrier. It began to crack, as evidenced by tendrils of light flaring across its surface. Sweat dripped down Alivia's face which contorted from exertion and strain. "Can't...hold..." she said, her voice sounding more normal. The black in her veins seemed to grow even darker, if that were possible, spreading wider and into the flesh surrounding them. She was killing herself.

"Alivia!" Emma shouted. "We have to go! You can't hold them!"

"Run," Alivia whispered. "Run. I will hold them off."

"No!" Emma said defiantly. "We are not leaving you behind again. Kylie, can you erect a smaller barrier behind Alivia's and leave it up for a time?"

"Yes."

"Then on three, erect the barrier and Alivia will drop hers. Then we run."

The others nodded their agreement.

"Three...two...one, now!"

She felt Kylie draw upon her magic and moments later she said, "Done!"

"Now, Alivia!" She waited a moment and felt the magic surging outward, then shoved her in the chest and felt a surge of power jolt down her arm. Black tendrils spread down her fingers, through her hand and began up her wrist. *Foreign presence detected. Activating defense matrix*, a voice came in her head, sounding like her own thoughts yet stiffer, like the voice in the void had been when she'd touched the orb. *Hello?* She thought, feeling silly. Of course no reply came. The black tendrils, much to her surprise and relief, had halted and were fading from view.

The push was enough for Alivia. The white faded from her eyes and she blinked. She lowered the staff but did not drop it. The black tendrils in her veins and skin remained but changed from night black to charcoal gray. "I..." she looked down at the staff in horror. "Yes, we have to go."

Emma led the retreat through the woods, light from the fire and lightning slamming against the barriers behind them competing with the sunlight to provide illumination. A boom and wave of pressure blasting through the undergrowth announced the destruction of Alivia's staff-induced barrier. All that remained was another, smaller boom and burst of pressure seconds later heralded the failure of Kylie's barrier. She ran all the faster, not daring to look back.

They ran until her legs ached and then kept running. She harbored no doubt Zerrecia and his Cult of Rae followers would be in hot pursuit. The woods thinned as a field appeared before her. They broke into the grassland and Emma halted, bending over to draw breath. The others took a cue from her and stopped also.

"Well, that was exhilarating," Favio said. "Now which way to throw them off our trail?" No one said anything. "Any ideas? The south, north, west? There are only three options."

"North," Alivia said as Emma spoke "south." They looked at each other. Alivia nodded to encourage Emma to speak.

"You told us we had to reach Tar Ebon. If we go south we can reach the road and follow it west." Why did she want to go north?

"Yes, I remember telling you that." She put a hand to her head.

"Then why do you want to go north? Are you feeling okay?"

"North there is..." she looked at Favio. "I thought if we went to Ironforge we might be safer. Safer until we can contact Tar Ebon. That's all."

"What is the staff doing to you?"

"Nothing you need worry about." She grunted. "I'm controlling it."

"It doesn't look you're doing a wonderful job of that," Favio pointed out.

"Hush, Favio," Emma said. "Will you..."

"What did you call him?" Alivia asked sharply, looking between Favio and Emma.

"Favio. He revealed his name during our stay in the dungeons."

"I must say prison changes a man," Favio said.

"What else did he tell you?" she asked warily.

Emma thought back. "Nothing." Now it was her turn to be suspicious. "Is there something..." A horn interrupted her. A horn from the east. "Bloodcloaks."

"We need to go, now," Ethan said, pointing out the obvious.

"Which way?" Kylie asked.

Alivia bowed her head. "I defer to you, Emma. My judgment is...compromised."

Thoughts whirred in Emma's mind. She attempted to conjure a mental picture of their location and how long it would take to reach the road versus Ironforge or a city to the west but the image disappeared as quickly as it came. Why hadn't she studied the maps closer? "The steam wagon. Could that plan still work?"

"Assuming *that* entire village isn't against us too," Favio added.

"It was ordered to remain there until I returned or sent word with instructions. It should still be there." Alivia struggled to speak, as if she were carrying a great weight. Emma sympathized, having touched the staff for only the briefest of moments. The memory of the voice speaking to her after touching the staff chose that moment to arise. *Were you real? Or just my imagination?*

I am "real" in the sense that I maintain a physical presence in your brain, the dull voice said.

Emma jumped.

"What's wrong?" Ethan said.

"Did you have a eureka moment?" Favio asked. "Perhaps an epiphany?"

Emma shook her head, annoyed by the intrusion. "No." *Who are you?*

I am a Neurological Interface Assistant.

What does that mean?

I interface with your brain to aid and support your nano-tech functions.

Emma's head spun. She had no idea what this assistant had said other than brain. *Nano-what? Neurological? Interface?* These were foreign words to her. *Where did you come from?*

I am uncertain. My physical placement suggests I have been present since birth, yet I only recently became active. My first recording shows you pushing a woman holding a staff as the genesis of a foreign presence I assisted in cleansing from your blood.

Oh. That made sense...sort of. She had first heard the voice after pushing Alivia. She shook her head. *We will talk later. I need to decide which way to go.*

Perhaps I can be of assistance, he said. She envisioned the implant being male, for his voice seemed too dull to her to be female. *What would you like to know?*

Emma hesitated. Perhaps she was hallucinating. She pinched her arm.

I assure you no hallucinogens are present in your blood.

Gee, thanks. I'm wasting time. Feeling silly, she continued. *I need to know where we are in relation to the steam wagon and the main road. Can you help with that?*

One moment, please. I am interfacing with the local mesh network. Again with the unfamiliar words.

Just hurry, please, Emma replied. She realized the others were looking at her strangely. "What?"

"Which way do we go?" Richard asked bluntly. "Or should one of us choose."

"Just let me think," Emma snapped, harsher than she meant to be. She inhaled deeply. "I'm sorry, just please, give me a moment." *What's the status?*

I have connected. Pulling up a virtual map of the region now. Her vision changed, much like it had when she'd touched the orb back at the fortress, and she found herself floating *above* the land. She saw her companions, and herself, below, looking like rabbits from the hawk's point of view. The vision continued outward until their group was but a speck below her. Forest stretched for miles in every direction. To the east the fortress they'd escaped from nestled up against the mountains, looking tiny in comparison. To the north smoke rose and words appeared there which read "Ironforge." To the west numerous villages were marked by names and far, far to the west a slim pillar rose, silhouetted against the even more distant mountains. A road ran to the south, a wide affair that dwarfed other roads. The King's Road.

She located Galdreth on the map in her mind, afraid to move beyond the point above her body. *I wonder how far Galdreth is compared to the King's Road.*

On foot Galdreth is three days walk. The King's Road is ten days walk.

Thank you, Emma said, her mind made up at last. "West," she said. "We go west to Galdreth and ride the steam wagon. We're closer to Galdreth than we are to the King's Road."

"And you know that how?" Ethan asked.

Emma hated lying to her brother but now was not the time to go talking about the voice in her head. "It's just a guess based upon how many days we've been traveling."

"I concur with her," Favio said. "I know something of the area from my time perusing maps while waiting to play chess with the king. This region of wilderness *is* quite distant from the King's Road."

"It's settled then," Alivia said, looking more haggard than before. "We go west. Lead the way."

Emma nodded, trying to look more confident than she felt. The reality of pursuers hot on their trail chose that moment to crash down on her. Fear entered her heart. What if the enemy caught up to them before they reached Galdreth? They had to make it. "Let's go." She headed westward.

What is your name?

I do not have a name? As I said, I am a...

Yeah, I got that part. Nia for short, but I don't like that name. She thought of the cat the neighbors had growing up. And he *was* shadowy. *I'll name you Shadow.*

I would be pleased to respond to such a wake word. Though I am always listening and ready to serve.

The thought of a voice in her head, an invisible assistant, listening to her thoughts caused Emma to shiver despite the warmth of the morning sun. *We're fortunate the weather has been mild for autumn,* she thought. *Without a coat I would be freezing right now if it were like normal.*

I can give you a weather report if you'd like. Would you like to know my prediction for the next week?

No, that's quite all right. Will you leave me to my thoughts for a bit? Please?

But of course. I am going to sleep now. Say the wake word of "Shadow" if you require my assistance.

Right. Wake word. Got it. She hummed, appreciating the silence in her head and focusing on the sounds of their footfalls as they moved through the tall grass. No wind interrupted their journey but the sound of a Bloodcloak horn did. It was closer...much closer. She turned to see a dozen or more Bloodcloaks on horseback riding out of the woods. "We've got company," she said.

The Bloodcloaks did not advance, like she expected. They milled about before disappearing into the woods. Emma frowned. "What are they doing?"

"They were a scout force," Richard said. "They're probably going back to report on our location. They wouldn't waste good horses charging across an open field knowing we have mages."

"He's right," Alivia said, sounding more like herself despite her affliction growing worse. "They will wait for the mages to support them before they attack. We need to reach the trees before they arrive so they don't have a clear line of sight."

The urgency in Emma's stride picked up now that they knew how close the enemy was. Part of her, not Shadow, said it would do no good to be exhausted when the enemy caught up to them. Emma told the pessimistic part of herself that if they pushed themselves they could possibly outrun the enemy. The enemy with horses...oh, right.

Trees stood perhaps a mile away when the earth began to shake. Emma halted. Several hundred feet in front of them the earth groaned and ripped apart, creating a rift between them and the forest. She groaned. They could still go north or south but their westward progress was halted. What were they going to do now?

"Get behind me," Alivia said. She clutched the staff in both hands and strode several feet toward where indiscernible figures in black robes stood. The dark mages had caught up. The Bloodcloaks, emboldened by the newcomers formed up ranks, obscuring the mages.

A fire ball streaked toward the group. Alivia raised her staff like she had before and the fireball split apart, raining fire onto the field below. A massive shard of ice followed. Alivia splintered it with a cyclone of wind she caused to envelope it. Lightning shot from her staff and flashed toward her foes. It hit an invisible barrier and spread across it like spider webs. A stalemate.

A second volley from the dark mages included fire, ice, wind and lightning at once. The individual attacks struck Alivia's barrier and broke against it, obscuring the casters of the magic.

The blackness continued spreading through Alivia as she cast her spells. It spread up the back of her neck. Emma ran around to the front of her and found it surrounding her eyes and spreading to her ears as well. "Alivia, you can't sustain this," she warned.

"I...must," Alivia said. She summoned fire, preparing to launch a massive fireball this time, when she collapsed. Her hand went to her head and she screamed in agony. She writhed in pain on the ground.

Emma knelt beside her but felt helpless as she continued to scream in agony. At last Alivia fell silent as unconsciousness took her.

Favio ran up to her and knelt.

Another burst of flame slammed against the barrier the arch mage had erected.

"Emma!" Ethan called. "The barrier!"

The barrier began to crackle like it had before. Without Alivia's consciousness sustaining it the construct would immediately become weaker. If it survived another strike they'd be lucky.

Emma ran back to the others. She spotted the staff and felt an urge to reach for it, to take it in her hands and use it to level the field of battle, literally or figuratively she didn't know. *No, I won't succumb*, she thought. Instead she said, "Link hands. We can combine our powers. Kylie, we'll use you as the focal point. Can you strengthen the barrier?" She pointed to the failing wall of energy.

"Yes, I can." Kylie held out her hand and smiled. "Let's do this as friends."

Emma took her hand. "As friends." Ethan took her other hand while Richard took Kylie's other hand. Favio hung back. An instant later she felt her power initiate and "channel" out of her into Kylie. Kylie became the focal point, like the prisms her father used to show her. She focused their individual streams of magic into a single beam. Then, being more powerful than any individual mage, they reinforced the barrier. The cracks of light mended and the barrier withstood the next attack from the dark mages, this in the form of dozens of fire balls.

"Time to strike back," Kylie growled. Perhaps the power was going to her head. She stretched her arms wide and the wind howled past Emma. It formed into a cyclone, towering above them and threatening to lift the mages off their feet. Kylie slapped her hands together and the cyclone moved forward, twisting as it went, as if her hand clap had propelled it forward. The cyclone reached the enemy barrier and almost broke through, for theirs shimmered with light and wind seemed to break through. But it held.

Kylie panted. "Tired," she said.

Emma felt exhaustion spreading through her too. Such a powerful attack drained the stamina of every member of the group.

The dark mages must have realized what the group was doing, for the next strike consisted of a massive lightning blast that continued to strike the shield in one spot. Zap, zap, zap went the cadence. Over and over the strikes went as the shield weakened. Emma felt waves of something assaulting her mind with each strike. It was taxing their magic to the core.

To Kylie's left, Richard let go of her hand and fainted. Immediately the pressure on Emma's mind increased as the streams of magic keeping the barrier intact diminished by one. The barrier reflected the weakening when the next burst, a massive fireball this time, spread across the entirety of the barrier and some flashed *through* the barrier.

Kylie grunted and redoubled her efforts. The barrier solidified but Kylie's grip on Emma's hand disappeared and she too fell to the ground. The link to the barrier shattered.

Emma clenched Ethan's hand harder and thought *we can do this, I know we can.* She looked her brother in the eye, then spotted the jewel atop the staff glowing. *There's no other option.* "The staff. I have to use the staff."

Ethan followed her gaze. "But it will destroy you, just like it did Alivia! And you don't know how to control your magic. Not completely."

"It's that or die," Emma argued. "And trust me, I don't think the staff will destroy me." He still wore a skeptical expression. "Please trust me, brother. I can do this."

"Not alone you're not." He squeezed her hand.

"Ethan. I can't risk you getting hurt."

He gave her a roguish grin reminiscent of their father. "I'm willing to take the risk. Trust me to do so."

Emma couldn't help but smile in return. If they died at least they would die together. "Favio, can you pull Kylie and Richard back?" She didn't wait for the bard's acknowledgment and led Ethan toward the staff. She bent down and seized it.

Energy surged through the staff up Emma's arm. Darkness crept up her hand but halted and retreated. *Foreign presence detected. Activating defense matrix,* Shadow blared in her head. *Foreign presence detected. Activating defense matrix.*

Can you shut off that warning? It's distracting?

Of course. Deactivating foreign presence alarm system. Note I am detecting short range communication from another implant of the same model as my unit.

Just now? Emma frowned. An odd time to mention something like that.

Yes. It is near.

Emma looked at Ethan. He wore a wide-eyed unfocused expression. The darkness spread into his left hand through Emma's right hand yet stopped. Just like her. Could he have an implant too? She didn't have time to ask him. The power of the staff flowed through her while her implant defended her against the corruption Alivia fell to. She still didn't understand much of it, but it didn't matter. Saving the lives of their companions did. She brought the staff in her left hand to a space in front of and between her and Ethan. He finally refocused his gaze and brought his right hand to grasp it also. It didn't add to the power she felt - they were already connected, but it seemed to lighten the pressure she felt running up her arm as her hand was no longer the sole conduit.

Together they raised the staff above their heads. Emma focused on the training they'd received from the witches. She closed her eyes and concentrated. There. She sensed the barrier and stretched her mind out toward it. She opened the door to her magic in her mind and it flooded down the connection to the barrier. Like a dam being broken the magic flooded the barrier, refilling and strengthening it. Another strike came, this of ice, and it shattered, sending ice shards toward the ground.

Emma felt her arm shaking. The power of the staff seemed endless but the human element, she and her brother, were not. Waves of exhaustion stronger than she'd felt earlier pounded her brain and racked her body. She funneled one last burst of energy into the barrier and felt something snap.

The orb atop the Staff of Agamar shattered, sending shard flying into the air and outward. Emma and Ethan dropped the staff and shielded their eyes as dark purple shards rained down on the battlefield.

The barrier flickered.

The dark mages, likely sensing weakness in their opponents, gathered their power. Energy crackled in the air around them and a moment later a beam of reddish yellow light washed against the barrier. It glowed before breaking, sending a wave of pressure outward.

Emma slumped, letting go of Ethan's hand. This was it - it was all over now. She looked her brother in the eyes. "I'm sorry." *I'm sorry I failed. I'm sorry I wasn't a better sister, I'm sorry I teased you.*

Ethan gave a wan smile this time, trying to be brave for her sake. He may not have been older than her as she was born several seconds before him, but he always tried to protect her, to stand up for her. He proved it again as he came to stand in front of her. As if his body could shield her from the inevitable blast coming next.

Chapter 18

The dark shards lying on the ground at that moment began to emit an eerie purple glow. Emma stood transfixed as dark mist the color of smoke rose from the earth across the battlefield. It obscured her view of the dark mages and made the field look as though it were on fire. The smoke took the shape of human figures, hundreds of them. Several hundred. More than Emma could comprehend in her exhausted state. The smoke solidified into flesh and armor and cloaks.

Standing before the twins, their backs to them, stood an army. Soldiers wearing black chest plates and helmets with shields in one hand and spears held upright in the other stretched north and south for half a mile. Figures of various height wearing cloaks with their hoods up formed a cluster near the middle of the formation but behind them. Some of the latter held objects like scepters, wands, rods or staffs. At the head of the soldiers a single distant figure sat atop a horse.

A pair of shadows appeared a few feet in front of Ethan and Emma. They resolved into a man and a woman.

The woman wore a black cloak with a hood up. Black trousers peeked out beneath the cloak. She assessed the twins with green eyes, her expression serious. Emma recognized her as the same woman from the void realm while communicating with the stone at the fortress.

The man, in contrast, wore navy breeches and a uniform with rank insignia upon it. A naval cap covered his head and he smiled at the twins, his blue eyes twinkling in the sunlight before looking toward where Alivia lay. He jogged over and knelt next to the fallen arch mage. Favio had returned to her side and he greeted the newcomer with a warm embrace before gesturing to Alivia, likely explaining what happened to her.

Behind the woman a horn blew. The soldiers lowered their spears in unison, letting out a "hoo" as they did. Fire arced from the direction of the dark mages, aiming to fall atop the army, but a counter-spell of ice slammed into it, sending water instead of deadly fire raining down on the soldiers.

"You held out," the woman before them said. "Good."

"How did you..." Emma said, unable to articulate her disbelief. Here she was, expecting to die at the hands of dark mages, and an army appears before her. "Where?"

The woman smirked. "I struck you speechless, I see. There will be time for explanations later." She pointed to the man in uniform. "That's my husband, Jason. He's a healer, among other things." She jerked a thumb over her shoulder. "That is the Iron Legion and some mages from Tar Ebon. We're here to stop that bastard Zerrecia."

Fire balls and ice arced from the mages of Tar Ebon toward the dark mages and their Bloodcloak servants. A vortex materialized on the far side of the battlefield and dark clouds threatened to block out the sun.

"And your name is?" Ethan asked.

"Bridgette. If you'll excuse me, I need to join the fight." She stepped back and her body faded to shadow. Seconds later she was gone, leaving a puff of smoke in her wake.

A second series of horns blasted. The mass of soldiers advanced, with the man on horseback raising his sword and pointing it toward the enemy. The soldiers raised their shields as arrows flew toward them from the Bloodcloaks. Archers at the rear of the army returned fire but their first volley turned to ash in midair. Emma did not know how many soldiers the Bloodcloaks had, but it seemed their dark mages were holding their own. A stray fireball broke through the defenses the Tar Ebon mages wove and struck a group of soldiers. Screams drifted on the wind.

"Come on, think," came an angry voice to Emma's left. Jason remained kneeling next to Alivia but smacked his forehead as he spoke. "What am I missing?" Favio stood off to the side, a worried expression on his face.

Emma, feeling helpless in the fight, limped over to the man. Ethan followed. "What's wrong?"

He spared them a quick glance before returning his gaze to study Alivia. "The radiation poisoning. My magic isn't affecting it. I've tried drawing it out, heating it, *cooling* it, running low level electricity through it. Nothing has worked."

"Electricity?" Ethan chose that moment to ask. As if there weren't more important things going on.

Jason waved his hands, perhaps grasping for an explanation. "Like lightning but on a much, much smaller scale."

"Oh."

"I don't know if this would help," Emma began hesitantly. "But what if it's not an energy inside her but a 'foreign presence?'"

Jason's head snapped up and he squinted at her. "Where did you hear that term?"

Emma's face went bright red. "Ummm...there's a voice...in my head," she realized how crazy that sounded the moment the words emerged. "When I touched the staff the voice said something about a foreign presence detected and activating a 'defense matrix.' I don't know what all that means but presence suggests a physical cause, yes?"

"I heard it too," Ethan said, stepping up beside her. "In my head."

"I didn't," Favio said. "If it matters."

Jason snapped his fingers. "Of course! It's not radiation it's a *virus*. Thank you, thank you, thank you." He turned back to Alivia and laid hands on her again.

He didn't even seem surprised, Emma thought. *Why didn't he even question us about hearing voices in our heads?* A question for a time when Alivia wasn't tangling from the precipice of oblivion.

She felt magic flowing from Jason into Alivia. She closed her eyes and observed waves of an unknown energy streaming into her. The waves ended abruptly.

Jason was shaking his head again. "I can *feel* the infection, but I can't affect it. It's too virulent." He paused. "Too strong."

"Can you see inside her body to gain a better understanding of it?" Emma asked. She had realized soon after they arrived that he was an Eternal, one of the strongest mages alive and a hero in the battle of Tar Ebon against the Krai'kesh. If anyone could see inside another person's body, not just sense things, it was him.

"No, I don't have an x-ray machine and...wait! Wait just a minute!" He leapt up and made it halfway to Emma, arms outstretched to hug her, before stopping. "Oh, sorry. But you're brilliant, absolutely brilliant!" He spread his arms wide. "We treat it like a cancer. We nuke it with concentrated radiation on a specific wavelength, much like x-ray or gamma. Well, not gamma, we don't want to fry her, but we have to find the perfect wavelength and power level."

What he'd said made no sense to Emma. She stared blankly at him. "I didn't understand any of that."

Jason waved a hand and ran back to Alivia. "There's plenty of time for learning, my dear. All you need to know right now is I *might* be able to save Alivia. If your parents instilled a belief in God within you, now is the time to pray."

The battle had devolved into a true battle like in the old story books now. Black-armored soldiers met with red-cloaked enemy combatants while the dead and wounded littered the ground between the archers and the rear of the Tar Ebon army. Spells continued to light up the sky and stimulate Emma's senses. Fire, ice, lightning and some elements of existence she did not recognize flew like archers exchanging arrow fire. Only far deadlier.

In the far distance the man atop the horse retained his position. He hacked around himself in a flurry so fast Emma could not follow it with her eyes. Dark clouds of mist billowed up from the enemy ranks. She caught a glimpse of a black cloak swirling among the red moments before two Bloodcloaks toppled to the ground. That had to be Bridgette, dealing death among them.

For Emma it was like seeing the stories come true. She'd read books and heard stories told by friends and townsfolk about the Eternals. Her father frequently warned her not to put stock in such tall tales. He mocked the idea that the Eternals stood ten-foot-tall and shot fire from their eyes, or that they could run faster than the wind and read minds. He maintained that they were ordinary people, like Emma and Ethan, with extraordinary magic. She hadn't always believed him and would often lay awake in her bed at night imagining what they would look like. She had to admit, based upon Jason, they did seem rather ordinary. Unless one counted eccentricity as a trait. Or brilliance, as Jason seemed highly intelligent.

"Are you watching?" Ethan asked, jostling her. He pointed to Jason.

"I'm trying to watch both," Emma said. "If we lose this battle it won't matter whether he succeeds or fails."

"We won't lose," Jason muttered absentmindedly. He held his hands about a foot away from Alivia's body. "Not with my wife and brother-in-law out there. Each are a one-man army, which makes it like a two-man army out there on top of a regular army. Poor saps don't stand a chance - they just haven't realized it yet."

"How is the treatment coming?" Emma asked.

"I've almost got it. I found just the right wavelength, basically the type of radiation, and am just playing around with the...bam, got it!" Energy built up in him and he almost seemed to glow. "Stand back, all of you! I don't want to risk sterility, though the risk is small."

"But you'll risk it in her?" Ethan asked.

"There isn't any other choice." He looked down at her and a melancholy expression overtook his face. "I'm sorry," he whispered. He placed both hands on Alivia's chest, right above her breasts, and the energy transferred through his arms into her body. The black infection beneath her skin and running through her veins reacted. It turned bright green and then yellow and finally faded, leaving her veins blue and her skin pale. He stood up, wobbling. "That takes a lot of energy. John would have been better suited for that."

"I hate to burst our bubble," Favio began, "but we have company." He pointed to the north where a group of Bloodcloaks approached on horseback. Their trajectory took them toward the mages of Tar Ebon. If they slaughtered them the Cult of Rae could turn the tides, regardless of how powerful Dawyn and Bridgette were. For their part, the mages were concentrating on the duel of death taking place above the clashing armies and seemed oblivious to the attackers coming from the rear.

"We have to warn them," Ethan said.

"We won't make it in time," Favio replied. "They'll be on them in seconds."

"Can you stop them?" Emma asked Jason.

The Eternal shook his head sadly. "I've used up my magic. I couldn't summon even a tiny breeze if my life depended on it. Not until I've rested. It's up to you."

Oh great, Emma thought. Up to the untrained mages. She could reinforce a construct of another mage, like the barrier, but could she stop dozens of mounted soldiers bearing down upon her fellow mages in time? A part of her doubted it. Still, she had to try. She looked to Ethan. "Are you up for one more try?"

He shrugged, a grim expression on his face. "We don't have a choice, do we?"

Her mother would say there's always a choice. Mostly in response to her or Ethan's excuses that they'd had no choice but to lie. She would say something about the right choice not always being the easiest choice and sometimes requiring the greatest sacrifice but there was *always* another choice. "There's only one right choice," she agreed. She held out her hand and he took it. "Let's do this."

Emma closed her eyes and grasped for the power inside her. She felt it, like a minuscule flame burning amid a thunderstorm - trying so hard not to be snuffed out. Her mind ached, her head throbbed, and her body threatened to give out on her. She shoved all those thoughts aside and in its place...emptiness. A void her mind floated in. She cupped the magic in her hand and, for the first time since their journey began, felt in control. It flowed through her, like water rushing through a dam. The world came alive with the smells of piss, shit, blood and living things now burnt; the sounds of screaming, shouting, dying soldiers and mages; the taste of blood and fire on the wind and the feel of ash drifting through her outstretched hand.

Her magic filled the space above her outstretched hand, drawing power from her brother, who had also managed to access his power, and focusing it into a single point. She opened her eyes a slit. A burning white-hot orb of fire floated inches above her skin. Pure heat, with the impurities burned away. Drawn from the bodies of the dead, from the grass bathed in sunlight, from the heated air above the melee - it all came to one compressed point. Light passed around it but when she tried to grasp the light it slipped from her control, like the frogs her brother used to catch. Then, in the space around the orb of compressed heat she evacuated the air, leaving a void around the flame. A barrier between it and the world. She pushed the heat from the void toward the center, leaving the air-less void around it colder than the coldest winter nights in the northernmost lands. The sunlight warmed the void, but she continued shoving every ounce of heat toward the center.

"Frostfire," she distantly heard Jason whisper with a hint of awe and exhaustion in his voice.

"Haven't seen that in twenty years," Favio said to him.

"Ashley would be proud."

Emma tuned them out, opened her eyes fully, and focused on the coming horsemen. They were seconds away from crashing into the mages, who were still oblivious to the impending doom. Or perhaps unable to drag themselves away from the fight long enough to fight them. That's where she came in. She sent the frostfire orb speeding toward a point in-between the horsemen and their prey. It sped through the air, leaving a trail of frost in its wake, like a person's breath in winter air. It came to rest a second later in the path of the enemy's advance.

One...two...three.

She unleashed part of the power contained in the condensed orb. The ground around the area froze in a flash, turning grass and dirt to a white-speckled wonderland. Just wide enough for the approaching horses, who could not stop. They slid across the ice and fell. A pile of horses and men grew. The last few rows of horsemen managed to stop in time.

The orb hovered above the clustered and now immobile soldiers, glowing bright white. *Part two.* She released her control on the flaming orb. A burst of light so bright she had to shield her eyes, followed by a wave of heat so intense she felt her hair might light on fire, exploded outward and down, directed by her will. The screams of the dying men and horses mingled together, turning into a high-pitched cacophony. The light from the explosion was replaced by burning foes, while the smell of blood gave way to the smell of burnt meat.

Emma gagged, her stomach heaving. In part because of the sight and smell, amplified due to her hold on her magic. In part from the thought that *she* had done this. She had slaughtered dozens of men in an instant. A hand on her shoulder brought her out of her painful trance. Ethan stood there, having released her hand. She smiled, remembering he was there, and embraced him. Waves of exhaustion she didn't know existed crashed into her. She slumped to the ground, her vision blackening before clearing. She feared she would pass out.

Would you like me to engage your adrenal system? Shadow asked.

She wanted to say no, assuming an adrenal system would keep unconsciousness at bay. She wanted to let unconsciousness take her, to fall asleep and wake in her bed back home, snug under her blankets. She prayed it was all a nightmare, a wonderful, terrible nightmare. Her eyes fell on Kylie and Richard, then went to Jason, Alivia and Favio. No, she didn't want this to be a dream. Despite everything - despite all the losses - she wouldn't trade the triumph she felt for anything. Wait till her parents saw her. *Just keep me awake, if you can.*

Cheers from ahead drew her attention. The soldiers cheered, lifting spears and swords high. The mages stood silent, subdued and likely exhausted. Had they won? She met Jason's eyes, imploring him silently.

He nodded. "It's over," he called from beside Alivia.

They'd won the day.

Post-battle clean up commenced, with the bodies of Tar Ebon's soldiers and the Bloodcloaks being stripped of their belongings and thrown in a heap. The pile burst into flame as several mages launched balls of fire at it.

Emma spent the time attending to Kylie and Richard, who remained unconscious. She forced them to take sips of water from Jason's canteen before taking a drink herself and offering it to Ethan. "You need to keep your strength up too."

"Do you have an...implant...too?" he asked, the word sounding foreign in his mouth.

She shrugged. "Apparently I do. It happened when I touched the staff."

"Me too," he said. He smiled. "It's pretty cool. Did you name yours?"

"Shadow."

"That's pretty cool. I named mine Frank."

Emma screwed up her nose. "Frank? What made you name it Frank?"

"Frank the baker," her brother replied, as if it should be obvious. "Because they sound the same."

"Ohhh," Emma said. "I hadn't thought of that." She laughed. "Shadow kind of sounds like him too. 'Hello, children, would you like some bread today,'" she said in an approximation of the stiff speech Shadow and Frank the baker shared.

Ethan laughed in turn, the exhaustion fading temporarily from his face. Their mother said laughter was the best medicine...she was right.

A gust of wind and something else, a force Emma couldn't put her finger on, like a burst of energy, from behind heralded the arrival of Bridgette. She appeared as if made of dark mist. Was she even human? She glanced at her husband and Alivia, nodded and approached the twins. "Quite a show you put on. Sent the enemy scampering away. Too bad Zerrecia and some of his cohorts escaped."

"Are you going to assault the fortress?" Emma asked. "They were capturing people with magic and converting them into cultists."

Bridgette looked over her shoulder. "That's his decision."

As if on cue, the man Emma saw earlier at the head of the Tar Ebon army approached on a massive black stallion. He removed his helmet, revealing short-cropped black hair. Two pairs of swords hung in sheaths at his side. He dismounted and bowed before her and Ethan. "The heroes of the battlefield, I presume."

Emma blushed. He was handsome, though she couldn't quite place his age. He reminded her of her father in that way. "We were hardly heroes. You and your army saved the day, not us."

He raised an eyebrow. "That's not what I heard. Bridgette tells me you reached out to her in the void, telling her of the Cult of Rae and their plans. You set this," he gestured to the army, "in motion."

Ethan elbowed her. "Just take the compliment. Who are you?"

"Ah, forgive me. My name is Dawyn Darklance. I am the supreme commander of the Black Guard."

"Black Guard?" Ethan asked.

"The name for the joint military forces of the Federation of Tar Ebon. I oversee it all. The army behind me is the First Legion."

"I'll ask my question to you, then," Emma began. "Are you going to attack Zerrecia's fortress?"

Dawyn sighed but offered a tired smile. "You are eager, aren't you? A warrior's spirit for certain. Right now we're tending to the wounded and burying the dead." A gust of wind brought the smell of burning flesh from the pyres burning in the distance. "But yes, we are going to assault Senegal Fortress." He looked at the ground where the shards of the Staff of Agamar lay. "I understand you destroyed the staff?" He didn't have to specify which.

"Not intentionally, but yes. During the fight, before you arrived."

He nodded. "It was once a powerful tool, but it became corrupt over the centuries. It's for the best you destroyed it."

Favio sauntered over. "What, you didn't want to say hello to me?" he pouted.

"Favio, you scoundrel." Dawyn smiled wide and shook hands with the bard. "I should have expected you to be at the center of the action."

"Oh, I wasn't," he said in a nonchalant tone, "I was back there fearing for my life."

Bridgette snorted. "Somehow I doubt that. You're a pragmatist, not a coward, Favio. You knew you couldn't fight their magic and you hung back." Her statement put things into perspective for Emma. She *had* wondered why he wasn't of more use during their escape attempts. Now she understood. He was playing to his strengths, like her father said he did as a shopkeeper.

Favio shrugged. "You know me too well."

"How is Alivia?" Dawyn asked, casting a concerned look toward the arch mage. She remained unconscious on the ground, though the black beneath her skin had disappeared.

"Jason says she will make a full recovery," Favio said. "This young lass helped with that too. Gave the mad scientist ideas for how to defeat the affliction. Speaking of you lassies, how is Isabelle, Bridgette?"

"Probably pacing aboard the ship, waiting for us to return. I told her to remain behind while Jason and I went to find him," she tipped her head toward Dawyn. "This place would have been too dangerous for a half-trained teenager."

Emma blinked. Bridgette had a daughter? A teenager too? Interesting.

Ethan found it interesting too, for he asked, "How old is your daughter?" a little *too* quickly.

Bridgette eyed him. "Down boy. She's your age. Sixteen. But she's definitely not your type."

Favio snickered, while Dawyn rolled his eyes.

How did she know their age? Maybe she guessed.

"I should get back," the supreme commander said. "I want the two of you to hang back during the assault on the fortress." He held up a finger to forestall her protest. "You've exhausted yourselves and look like you're running on fumes. Low on energy," he explained when he saw their confused looks. "Stay here with the camp and rest. Do you promise you'll do that?"

Emma had no other choice but to nod. Ethan followed suit.

Chapter 19

E mma looked out the flap of the tent she and the others occupied. The rearguard of the army maintained a perimeter, but the rest of the army was long gone.

After Dawyn returned to his army, Bridgette had disappeared into the void to fetch the supply chain for the army, including supply wagons carrying tents. The supreme commander had lent his own tent for the use of Emma and her companions.

Inside, Richard, Kylie and Alivia lay in a row, still unconscious. Favio lounged in a chair, picking his teeth with the tip of a knife. Ethan brooded, yes, brooded, next to the bard. Favio's charm didn't seem to affect him today. She tried to think what he had to brood about. He hadn't wanted to leave Ironforge. Was he mad they couldn't return home? Or was he still mourning the loss of Jasmine? To Emma, the night they lost Jasmine seemed ages ago. It felt like they'd been traveling for an eternity, even though it had only been days.

"Are your wardens out there?" Favio asked.

"I thought you were our warden," Emma shot back.

He smirked. "Hardly. I'm not that trustworthy."

"They're still there."

As if they knew who she referred to, one of the mages standing outside their tent looked at her. His blond hair reflected the midday sun. He did not smile. Perhaps he was upset being on what one could consider "babysitting duty" instead of being with the main assault force. The gods knew any army assaulting Senegal Fortress would need all the help they could get. Which made sitting around waiting even more frustrating in Emma's eyes. Just the memory of the power she'd wielded only hours before sent chills down her spine.

"Too bad, eh Ethan?" Favio said, nudging her brother.

He returned the gesture with a glare. "We're being treated like criminals."

"We are not," Emma protested. "Do you want more enemies to slip into camp and kill us while we're powerless?" She may not have liked being stuck there but she did understand the reasoning behind Dawyn ordering them to remain behind.

Ethan shrugged and averted his eyes. "Whatever."

The phrase made Emma's blood boil. It was a phrase their father used toward their mother at his peril, often ending with one or both storming from the room in anger. It had a similar effect on her in that moment, causing her to clench her fists and swallow hard to avoid shouting. She turned around so as not to see his face and a groan from the direction of her unconscious friends relieved her of the desire to produce an angry response to her brother. "One of them is awake," she said instead.

Indeed, Kylie sat up, rubbing her head. "Water," she croaked, her voice barely audible.

"Right," Emma said, starting and hurrying to the bucket of fresh water near the side of the tent. Using a large cup, she gathered a large amount of water for her friend. She held the cup up to her lips and the girl slurped gratefully.

"What, where," Kylie began after she'd swallowed her fill. She put a hand to her head, then pinched her arm. "Am I dreaming? Hallucinating? Are we dead and in the Celestial Halls?"

Emma laughed. "You're none of those things." She recounted the tale of their rescue for the next several minutes. She finished with, "and now we're stuck in here waiting for you all to wake up and for the army to assault Senegal Fortress."

"I'm surprised Alivia survived. The ancient texts tell that when the staff was held for too long by a person not equipped to wield it death was certain."

"It would have been for her, too, if not for Jason."

"I still can't believe you met an Eternal."

"Three Eternals," Emma corrected. "Remember?"

"Oh yeah. My memory is still a little...fuzzy."

"I understand." Emma put a hand on her friend's shoulder. "You're going to be just fine. We'll be to the Tower in no time."

A boom to the east sent a shudder through the ground and Emma struggled to maintain her balance.

"What was that?" Ethan asked.

Emma went to the door of the tent and peeked out. Deep dark billowing smoke rose from the east. "What was that?" she repeated her brother's question to the mages outside.

"The assault has likely begun," the blond-haired mage said. The gray-haired woman opposite him didn't respond to her query.

"Can we come out and watch?" she asked.

The man hesitated, pursing his lips. He glanced at the woman. She still did not acknowledge him. She sighed. "Yes, you can come out. But stay in sight of us, you hear?"

"Of course," Emma said, injecting as much innocence as possible into her voice to convince the guard of her sincerity. She returned to the interior of the tent and informed the others they could come out. Minutes later she and the three conscious members of her party stood watching yet more smoke seeping into the sky.

"What kind of magic creates that much smoke?" Ethan asked.

"Perhaps they're having a large barbecue," Favio offered.

"Hopefully not with Federation troops," the female mage said.

In that moment the smoke twisted around itself and stretched toward the clouds. It widened at the top and narrowed toward the bottom. It rotated faster and a high-pitched howling began.

"Cyclone," Kylie said. "Powerful wind magic."

Emma stood transfixed, unable to take her eyes off the massive cyclone forming in the direction of the fortress. "Who could create such a thing?"

"Jason could," Favio said. When the other three turned to look at him, he shrugged. "What? I may know nothing about magic, but I do know what that man is capable of. During the battle for Tar Ebon he summoned dozens of tornadoes, er, cyclones, at once."

"That still doesn't answer what caused the smoke," Emma said.

"Ethan, Emma?" Richard called from within the tent. "Where are you guys?"

Emma popped her head into the tent. "We're out here. Are you all right?"

Richard stood there, naked from the waist up, his muscles no longer relaxed from sleep and making her blush for staring at his body too long. "I'm still feeling light-headed," he said, "and hungry." He put a hand on his stomach hidden by abs.

"Come out here. I think we can help with that." She led her comrade, clothed with a shirt now, out to the others.

The massive cyclone moved north and south, and perhaps west a little, before dissolving minutes later. Would such a thing have damaged the fortress? What if it hadn't been the Federation who created it? A surge of fear filled her.

Her fears were assuaged an hour later, during which they fed Richard and filled him in on what he'd missed. The army once again emerged from the woods, reminding her of the Bloodcloaks emerging earlier that day. There were noticeably fewer soldiers, which drew mutters from the gray-haired mage behind her.

Bridgette and Jason approached their tent. Ash and blood covered her grim face, while he appeared exhausted.

"What happened?" Emma asked.

"A bloodbath. The Bloodcloaks and the Cult of Rae were entrenched. More than we expected."

"We told you everything we knew," Emma said, hoping they wouldn't be blamed for the slaughter.

Bridgette shook her head. "It wasn't your fault. Zerrecia outsmarted us and would have won if Jason hadn't turned his magic against him."

"The smoke," Emma guessed.

"An oil pit," Bridgette explained. "He lit it on fire once our soldiers were in the middle. I got as many as I could out, and the mages tried to fight it, but..." For the first time in the brief time Emma had known the woman she was struck speechless.

"The oil burned at too high of a temperature for it to be cooled down quickly enough with traditional means," Jason took over. He didn't quite have a dispassionate voice but more like what Emma associated with Shadow. "So I used a tornado to rapidly suck the heat up as it was generated and funnel it into the clouds where it cooled. We're likely to see rain soon." Indeed, the clouds were looking darker, even threatening to block out the sun.

"Still. So many lives lost," Emma said.

"Did you kill Zerrecia?" Alivia asked, causing Emma to jump. She hadn't heard the arch mage arise.

Bridgette smiled thinly in greeting before frowning. "No, he wasn't there."

"He left his people there to die?" Ethan asked.

"The mages are fanatics. In their eyes they would give everything, including their lives, for their leader. As for the Bloodcloaks - they probably didn't even notice his absence."

"At least it lays in ruins now," Jason said. He shivered. "It was an evil place."

"Thank you," Alivia said. She looked to Emma and her companions. "I sense there's a story behind all of this and him." She gestured to the approaching army and the supreme commander, who approached on his stallion.

"A long story," Emma said, smiling in relief.

Chapter 20

Hours later, after the tale of their survival and exploits during the battle had been recounted at least once, with several parts being retold many times, Dawyn leaned back in his chair. "So, are you going to take the steam wagon or let Bridgette transport you?"

Alivia sighed. "I hope you won't be offended, Jason, but I do prefer shifting to the steam wagon."

Jason laughed. "No offense taken. Trust me, what we've got cooking up right now will revolutionize transportation even more than the steam wagon."

"More?" she asked, incredulous. "How much more could you revolutionize things?"

"A lot more," Dawyn said. "More than you can imagine. But it takes moving one step at a time. We must never take our eyes off the goal." It sounded to Emma as though he was speaking for the benefit of Jason and Bridgette, not for the others in the tent, for they both nodded in understanding.

"We're preparing to shift in a few minutes," Bridgette said. "Gather your things."

Emma and her friends set about gathering their meager possessions. The tent came down minutes later to be packed into a cart, revealing the remains of the army bustling with activity as they broke their hasty camp. Rain fell, as Jason had predicted, though it was not heavy yet.

"How does your shifting work?" Emma asked her.

"I require a living person on or within something to transport it. Their...live essence, I guess you would call it, is how I locate them. I can sometimes locate them in other ways, such as when you caused the explosion of the Staff of Agamar. That set off a veritable beacon in the shadow realm."

"Would you have found us if we hadn't used the staff?"

"Perhaps, but we could have shifted in miles from here. I might not have known exactly where you were. We could have shifted in at the fortress or just outside it and missed you."

The army formed up ranks. Alivia led Emma and the others to the rear where the remaining mages of Tar Ebon stood. Jason and Bridgette joined them.

"Here we go," Bridgette said. She closed her eyes and Emma felt a force tugging at her. Her skin became transparent and a second later the landscape turned to a shadow of itself. *This must be the shadow realm*, she thought.

Bridgette did not give her much time to appreciate the scenery, or lack thereof. *Blink*. The landscape changed to rolling hills. A road ran to their left. *Blink*. It changed again, this time they straddled a cliff overlooking a river valley. *Blink*. They stood on an open field, hills behind them and a massive city in front of them with dark walls rising impossibly high. There, dwarfing the walls and all other buildings, stood a massive square-sided building. That had to be it. It had to be the Tower of the Seven Stars.

The shadow realm faded and Emma's body returned to flesh. Color returned to the sights and made the Tower look more resplendent than it already looked.

"Welcome home," Alivia said, gesturing, as if they couldn't see the massive structures ahead of them. "Welcome to Tar Ebon."

The army formed into columns and marched toward the city gates, which were creaking open. The mages formed up at the rear of the last infantry column, preparing to enter after.

Emma turned eastward, straining to see any sign of the smoke that had risen from the fortress, or even the dark clouds produced by Jason's magic. She saw no sign of it. How far they had traveled in moments. Amazing.

"Well, this is goodbye," Bridgette said. "We have to get back to the ship." She cleared her throat. "I'm sure we'll meet again one day."

Jason stepped forward, eager to shake Ethan and Emma's hands. "You two are destined for greatness, I just know it."

"Thanks," Emma said hesitantly. "But we've just started our training."

"Training can be overrated," he replied, glancing at Alivia and smiling. "But you have one of the best teachers overseeing your training here. You're in good hands."

"Thank you for everything, again," Alivia said.

Jason bowed, Bridgette shifted, and they were gone.

Emma let out a deep sigh. It was over. It was finally over. They'd taken "the long way 'round," as her father would say, but they'd made it. She stared up at the top of the Tower, which stood well above the looming black walls of the city. What secrets, what wonders, awaited them there?

THE END

Connect with the Author:

The author loves to connect with fans. You can reach him through any of these methods:

1. Email him at admin@darkstarpublishing.com

2. Visit his Facebook page at https://www.facebook.com/SagaOfTheSevenStars[1]/ and give his page a like.

3. Follow him on Twitter. His handle is @dayne87

Other Books in the Seven Stars Universe

The Shadow Trilogy (Fantasy)

1. Blood and Shadows
2. Time of Shadows
3. Shadows Fall

The Mageborn Saga (Fantasy)

1. Mageborn (this book)
2. The Cursed Tower (May 2018)
3. Halls of Light (2019)

The Dark Tide Trilogy (Space Opera)

1. Emergence
2. Eclipse
3. Ruin

Review This Book and Receive a Free Copy of the Next

IF YOU REVIEW THIS book and leave a review on your favorite public site and send me a link to it as proof, you will receive a free copy of my books once they are finished!

Just email proof of your review (a link to where it's posted) to admin@darkstarpublishing.com. Thanks!

The Cursed Tower Excerpt (Available Now)

Emma raced through the forest. She winced as she brushed a thorn bush, causing a cut on her forearm. Her chest heaved as she ignored the pain and leapt over a log. A vicious roar from behind shook the leaves around her. She had to keep going, though she didn't know why. It will kill me, she thought, though she couldn't remember what "it" was. Still she ran. Run was the sole thought in her mind. An overriding thought disallowing any other thoughts to intrude for long.

The forest ended abruptly, as if the land were sliced by a knife. Before her lay an arena. Without thought she ran into the gritty sand, then turned around. The forest was gone, replaced by a brick wall. What forest? She held a sword in one hand and a shield in the other, though she couldn't remember how they came to be there. Something didn't feel right, but she couldn't put her finger on it. It was like trying to hold a fish, a lesson she'd learned the one time her father took she and Ethan fishing near Ironforge. The memory of that day when she'd caught a fish and tried snatching it appeared and disappeared, replaced with fear once more as the thing approached from behind a large wooden door on the other side of the arena. The door shattered, sending splinters flying across the arena. Emma raised her shield and felt and heard the impact of shards against it.

She lowered the shield and beheld a monster. The creature with red skin, standing twice as tall as her brother, stood on two hoofed feet, had the torso and arms of a man and the head of a bull, with horns arcing out and pointed skyward. It held a double-bladed axe in its massive hands. It threw back its head and bellowed, causing the arena to shake. Emma quivered in fear, her hands threatening to drop the sword and shield. How could she stand against such a thing?

Use magic, a voice in her head said. Magic? She didn't possess magic. No, all she had were mundane weapons. She was going to die. It would all be for nothing. Her family would...did she have a family? She couldn't remember.

The bull-man interrupted her ruminations by pawing at the ground, lowering its head and charging. Dust streamed behind him and he raised his axe as he ran.

Emma raised her shield, preparing for a strike. Wait, she, a sixteen-year-old girl, couldn't stand against a blow from such a beast. What was she thinking? She tossed the shield aside and ran toward the monster. Something inside told her the best chance for survival was to be faster than the beast. When she was a few feet away her opponent swung his axe. She changed her speed and dodged the strike, coming up behind it. She slashed at his calf and felt the sword hit home, slicing through flesh and hitting bone.

The creature roared in anger and limped, turning toward her. It took a step and stumbled before catching itself. But it's axe slipped from its grip and slid to the ground. It struggled to take another step but roared in pain and collapsed under its weight.

Emma stepped forward cautiously and kicked the axe behind her. Then she crept toward the man-bull and raised her sword. Now was the moment. No, a voice said in the back of her mind. A mage is merciful.

I'm not a mage! she shouted back in her mind. Here she was, arguing with herself about morality. Where had she gotten such a delusion from?

Still, she didn't lower the sword. It shook in her hands as her mind said thrust and her body refused. She blinked and studied her opponent.

The creature moaned in pain, it's ferocity gone. But it would have had no qualms about murdering her. Wait, what was that? She leaned closer, holding the sword to the side. A collar around its neck. Was it a slave? Maybe it was attacking her at its master's command. She bit her lip and raised the sword again. She slammed it down. Clang, the iron shattered, and the collar fell in pieces to the ground.

Shocked expression on its face, the creature looked up at her. It groaned in a different tone, one reminiscent of a question. "Why?" The tone seemed to ask.

"Because you are not my enemy," she said, casting the sword aside and feeling braver than she ever recalled being, which wasn't saying much.

She turned around, intending to walk away.

The landscape changed. She stood before a golden door. She looked behind her, but the sand and the monster were gone. Had they ever really been there?

"Ah, a visitor," a voice came from behind.

Emma spun to find a giant golden cat of some sort sitting in front of her. Its green eyes studied Emma. "What are you?" She asked, tensing and wishing she possessed a weapon. Hadn't she had one? She put a hand to her head. It was so difficult to remember.

"I am the Sphinx," it replied.

"Why are you here?"

"To test you, child. Answer my riddle correctly and you may choose a door. Answer it incorrectly and you shall face death."

"Death from what?" Emma asked. She didn't see anything around.

"Why, from me, my dear." The Sphinx stretched and opened its mouth wide, revealing two rows of jagged, sharp teeth. "Are you ready?"

Emma swallowed. She didn't have a choice. "Yes."

Buy The Cursed Tower Now at this link.[2]

---

2. https://www.books2read.com/u/4AwZwN

Don't miss out!

Visit the website below and you can sign up to receive emails whenever Dayne Edmondson publishes a new book. There's no charge and no obligation.

https://books2read.com/r/B-A-ZEND-SJRR

BOOKS 2 READ

Connecting independent readers to independent writers.

Did you love *Mageborn*? Then you should read *The Cursed Tower* by Dayne Edmondson!

The Cult of Rae have infiltrated the Tower of the Seven Stars and **doom could follow them.**

Emma and her brother and friends have arrived at the Tower of the Seven Stars to begin their formal magical training. But their training is cut short when they uncover a plot by the nefarious Cult of Rae to bring the Tower crumbling down.

Can Emma and her friends investigate the strange happenings at the Tower while keeping up with their schoolwork and nursing new rivalries? And do they have the magical prowess to stand against the cultists? If not, the entire Tower, and later the world, could come to a tragic end.

Another installment in the Seven Stars Universe by Dayne Edmondson, this is a young adult fantasy novel set twenty years after "Shadows Fall" and featuring cameos from some famous characters.

Buy now to jump into the adventure.

Read more at https://www.darkstarpublishing.com.

Also by Dayne Edmondson

The Dark Tide Trilogy
Emergence
Eclipse
Ruin

The Mageborn Saga
Mageborn
The Cursed Tower
Halls of Light

The Seven Stars Universe
Ghost Ranger
Space Commando

The Shadow Trilogy
Blood and Shadows
Time of Shadows
Shadows Fall

Standalone
The Complete Dark Tide Trilogy
The Complete Shadow Trilogy

Watch for more at https://www.darkstarpublishing.com.

About the Author

Dayne Edmondson lives in southeastern Michigan with his wife and two young children, a boy and a girl. He writes part time and works a day job.

His books can be read in this order:

The Shadow Trilogy:

1. Blood and Shadows
2. Time of Shadows
3. Shadows Fall

Mageborn Saga:

1. Mageborn
2. The Cursed Tower
3. Halls of Light (coming 2019)

The Seven Stars Universe:

1. Ghost Ranger (coming 2019)

The Dark Tide Trilogy:

1. Emergence
2. Eclipse
3. Ruin

Dayne enjoys reading, writing, the occasional video game, watching TV with his wife, walking and spending time with his children indoors or out.

He writes and reads science fiction and fantasy. Some of his favorite authors/books include Robert Jordan, Brandon Sanderson, (almost) all the Star Wars EU books, Elizabeth Haydon, Christopher Nuttall and more.

Read more at https://www.darkstarpublishing.com.

About the Publisher

Dark Star Publishing is a small-press publisher of science fiction and fantasy novels. They place particular emphasis on books written **in** the Seven Stars Universe (the universe created by author and owner Dayne Edmondson).

For more information, visit https://www.darkstarpublishing.com